SEAM OF GOLD

WATERPATHS SAGA #1

LUCY HOLDEN

FEHU PRESS

*For the Happy Girls
with bubbles, love, and joy.*

FOREWORD

Readers of the Nightgarden Saga will be aware of many of the events that precede this book, as if follows directly on from that series and the follow up book, Fleur de Lis. The Waterpaths Saga also links to the events in the fantasy romance world in the Woven Saga.

You don't have to read any other books to enjoy this series, but if you wish to, the order of previous books is as follows:

NIGHTGARDEN SAGA

1. Prequel to the Nightgarden Saga (free download)
2. Red Magnolia
3. Moonvine
4. Poison Berry
5. Bayou Rose
6. Dusky Dahlia
7. Blue Lilies
8. Night Shade
9. Fleur de Lis (free download)

WOVEN SAGA
1. Woven in Darkness
2. Woven in Savagery (coming 2024).

PROLOGUE

ANTOINE

*D*ear Jeremiah,

That is no longer your name, but it is the one by which I remember you. Perhaps it is a mark of insanity that I write these letters, knowing you will never see them. Even if you lived a long life, you have been dead now for at least one hundred and fifty years, though I can find no record of it anywhere—and I am adept in such matters.

I write because you are the only one who knows the answers to the questions that haunt my every waking moment. And even if I cannot ask them of you in person, writing them down helps me keep the fears at bay, temporarily at least.

Time passes differently for the immortal. At first, I reveled in that. Then I went through the inevitable years of cursing it, until I found Harper, and learned I would share eternity with her. It seemed an almost incomprehensible gift.

But that was before we had time traveling twin girls and were forced to reckon with the terrible irony that they may not share that eternity with us.

In a cruel twist of fate, our daughters age faster than mortals, simply because they live so many days in distant times. Their twenty first birthday is next week. Their passports say they are thirty, though for some time now their appearance seems to have been arrested somewhere around the mid-twenties. But do I trust that they will remain that age, Jeremiah? How can I, when even their conception is a mystery? And how does one test for immortality—other than facing death itself?

They heal quickly, that much we know. And their aging has certainly slowed. But healing is not immortality, and we don't know how long the aging will be arrested. Wolves heal fast, yet they can be killed. There are no textbooks on supernatural lifespans. What evidence may exist is carefully disguised in old grimoires, or books considered to be fairy tales by others. Modern science offers little help. I've compelled scientists and clinics beyond measure in my search for answers, but none have shed any light on our questions.

Harper and I could give the girls our blood, of course. Could turn them into vampires ourselves. But neither of us know what creatures they might become if we do. Would they survive? Would they become something none of us have ever seen before? Would they still travel the waterpaths? If I thought it would save their lives, I would change them in an instant, and damn the consequences. But the truth is that transitioning to vampire form is dangerous at the best of times. Aurelia and Marguerite were born magical. Attempting to change them with more supernatural power seems a direct challenge to whatever gods any of us might still believe in. I am not at all certain it is our place to change whatever course fate has dictated for them.

Perhaps, if they lived gentle lives under my protection, I would find that easier to live with.

But they are both as stubborn as I ever was, in their own ways. And neither has chosen an easy path.

They are living in Granada now, in a house their uncle Connor restored. It is beautiful, a 16th century Moorish carmen on the medieval hillside of the Albaicin. Pomegranate and fig trees drop fruit over the whitewashed walls, and jasmine twines with citron by the fountain in the internal courtyard. The terrace looks across the valley to the ochre walls of the Alhambra palaces.

But I need not tell you any of this. You once lived in that very carmen. You and I once sat on that same terrace, sharing a bottle of red wine as the moon rose over the palaces. You know well why I do not love the Alhambra's beauty. It is hard to love a place in which one was imprisoned, and almost died.

What is harder is that I cannot tell my daughters of that past. I do not even tell Harper of that time. My shock, when first I realized which house Connor meant to restore, was so great I had to remove myself for several days on the pretext of business. He had no idea, of course. None of them do. But can such a coincidence be chance, Jeremiah? How is it that fate should place my daughters in the very house once occupied by El Viajero, arguably the greatest, if largely unknown, spy master of the Napoleonic age? How is it that they are living in the very house inhabited by you, Callie, and your daughter, all those years ago, the same place in which I took refuge after my ordeal?

I have a terrible feeling of time loops closing, of past and present reaching for each other. I might feel excited about that, if I did not know just how brutal that past was—and if it wasn't for the careers my daughters have chosen.

Modern parenting, Jeremiah. It is enough to make me long for the days of corsets and patriarchy. (Never tell Harper I said that.)

Marguerite is a lecturer in archeology at the University of Granada. It is easy, it seems, to earn doctorates and professional accolades when one can live two lives at once. She had her PhD by the time she was officially eighteen and is now a renowned expert in Granada's architectural history. She did her dissertation on the Alhambra, the very place where I once endured prison and torture.

If that does not already fill you with alarm, Aurelia's path certainly should: she joined the Spanish army several years ago and is now part of their Special Operations Group. It seems the Spaniards are as willing to accept women in active service as they were back when female *guerilleros* fought against Napoleon. Most countries are wary of taking women into their elite units. Not Spain. They merrily send them off to theatres of war in delightful places like North Africa and the Middle East. Apparently, women are an 'advantage' in such environments.

An advantage.

If vampires could age, Jeremiah, I would wear every one of my three hundred years on my face.

The worst of it is that I know exactly why the twins have chosen those careers. Of all the periods in history they have traveled to, the waterpaths leading to one have remained steadfastly closed to them: the years between 1793 and 1824. The French Revolution, where we believe you traveled when you left us. Napoleon's war on Spain, in which you were so instrumental. And the London Regency period, when I believe, though I cannot be certain, that I once met your daughter.

I know this only because when the girls were younger, before they learned to hide their travels from Harper and I, they read the Scarlet Pimpernel, and decided to go back and have a look at the French Revolution for themselves. When they couldn't get there, they came to us, quite indignant that a waterpath should be closed to them. The mere thought of them landing in Paris somewhere amid that period of blood and savagery made me feel so helpless that I confess my reaction was less . . .measured, than it could have been. I strictly forbade them from even attempting to travel anywhere near that era, and Harper and I ceased speaking about you and Callie at all. In fact, we shut down any discussion about the events surrounding their birth, or the people involved in them. It seemed to me that those waterpaths must be closed to them for a reason, and I saw no reason to tempt fate.

It was only as the years played out and the girls made their career choices that it began to become clear to me that they never had any intention of letting those mysteries lie.

I know they are in Granada because they want to try to find you and Callie, or at least discover what became of you. I guess it is natural, given that you are the only ones who might have answers to their questions about their own mortality, and about what magic lives in the pendants they both wear. The topic of immortality has long been a closed one in our household, but that doesn't mean they don't think about it just as much as Harper and I do. Probably more. I fear they have dared death on multiple occasions, particularly Aurelia, just to test their own mortality. I try not to think about it.

Try.

But you and I know the horror of Napoleon's war on Spain, Jeremiah. The savagery of the invading French forces, and the suffering of the Spanish as they fought for independence against the Napoleonic regime. The thought of my girls finding themselves amidst that chaos terrifies me beyond all reason.

Which brings me back to my initial cruel twist of fate.

My girls seem hell bent on throwing themselves into the path of danger. We do not know if they are truly immortal, nor what they may be vulnerable to. Am I supposed to simply stand by, Jeremiah, knowing they are trying everything they can to find their way back to one of history's most brutal times? Stand by as they both dare death, Aurelia by entering theatres of war that most men hesitate to go and Marguerite by visiting sites and handling artefacts that can transport her into times and places even I would not wish to revisit?

Do Harper and I change them into vampires, and risk the unknown consequences? Our own blood has notorious powers beyond merely being vampiric. Mine has made wolves immortal and activated powers in others. Harper's blood was powerful enough to cause me to father children when I should technically have been dead. What might our blood activate in our own children? And what if our girls wish to have children of their own? How dare we deprive them of the chance to at least try that?

But Jeremiah, please explain to me how, as a father and an immortal who has seen more suffering and death than most ever will, I can stand aside and simply wait to discover if my daughters will live, or die?

For I cannot follow them into the past. And nor can I guard their present every waking moment, not without losing them.

This life I once thought a precious gift is fast becoming an exquisite agony, Jeremiah. One I have no idea how to escape.

Tomorrow Harper and I will arrive in Granada for the twins' birthday celebrations. Hard conversations must be had, ones I dread, but they cannot be postponed for another day.

Too much rests upon the decisions we make.

I wish you, of all people, were here, Jeremiah. I feel you would have the answers I seek. And I will not lie—you, who of all people knew the uncertainty we must surely have to face— why did you not leave me some kind of reassurance? Why did you leave no trace of what happened to you?

Do you know something that I do not?

Such questions torment me beyond sleep tonight. And so, I will run and lose myself in the hunt, that when I return to Harper's bed, she may not know the agonies I have felt in these thoughts.

~

Yours,
Antoine Marigny.

CHAPTER 1

RETURNING

Antoine

"I know you don't like being here." Harper's hand closes over mine. I stare out of the airplane window, reluctant to meet her eyes. Harper always sees what others don't.

"I'm fine." I squeeze her hand without turning. Below, the snowcapped mountains of Spain's Sierra Nevada gleam in the midday sun. They rarely lose their mantle of white, even in midsummer. In April they are still liberally covered. The airport is on the plains, in the modern part of the city, which is as grim and industrial as any other twentieth-century urban center. My eyes are fixed on the twin hills of the older part, divided by the river Darro. On the eastern side of the valley the ancient palaces of the Alhambra sprawl across one hillside. On the other side, a tumble of whitewashed houses mark the medieval suburb of the Albaicin. Both have origins dating back to the Romans, though the height of their construction occurred after the tenth century, when the Moorish kings ruled Granada and built the magnificent Nasrid palaces that are still the centerpiece of the Alhambra.

"I wish we could have held the twins' party in Mississippi." I turn at the note of longing in Harper's voice. The midmorning light turns her long auburn curls to blazing fire.

"You know that is impossible." I touch her face, tracing the porcelain features frozen into eternal perfection. Her beauty catches my breath, even now, over twenty years since we met, but it is in the emerald depths of her eyes that I am truly lost. Immortal bodies might remain untouched by the ravages of time, but the eyes always betray the soul within. Harper has seen more of death and trial than most humans could ever know. Yet still she loves fiercely and without compromise.

At least she does now. What if the worst is yet to come? Will I be forced to watch the light fade from those eyes, replaced by the emptiness of an eternity lived without our twins?

I push away the traitorous thoughts and force a smile. "The Marigny family name might have been temporarily restored to some form of normality when the girls were young. But even if we could feasibly present them to Deepwater Hollow again as adults without too much remark, nothing can explain away the fact that you and I haven't aged a day. People were already beginning to look at us askance when we left for France."

"I know that." Harper looks away from me, her tone resigned. "I understand why we had to leave, just as I understood when we left France, and later, Italy. Just as I understand why we don't make friends in England, and why the girls have chosen to live here." She turns back to me, her eyes sad and full of love all at once. "But understanding doesn't make it any easier to accept."

We have conducted our conversation in a sub whisper heard only by preternatural ears. I catch a woman on the neighboring row eyeing us curiously, and say in a slightly louder voice, "I'm looking forward to meeting our friends again."

The woman leans forward. "Is it your first time traveling to Granada?" Taking in our wedding rings, she bestows an indulgent smile on us both. "I remember when I was young and newly married. Such fun days. And you should travel as much as you can, before you settle down, and have children."

I stifle a grin. Harper grips my hand warningly. "Yes," she says, with a brilliant smile. "We're catching up with old friends who live here. It's been a long time."

"Oh, you must make sure you visit the Alhambra while you're here." The woman goes on to explain how we might go about buying tickets to see the palaces. We nod along, as if we can't simply leap the wall after dark and roam the palaces at our leisure.

Not that we will. I suppress a shudder at the thought of venturing behind those walls again. I've never spoken about my time here at length to anyone, not even Harper. Part of me hoped that my silence on the topic would help our daughters grow out of their seeming obsession with Granada, and the Napoleonic era in general. Which is yet more proof, if ever I needed it, of how little I understand about parenting.

The plane's landing gear cuts off the conversation and my thoughts. We leave the airport and I give swift instructions to a cab driver in Spanish. Harper's hand remains tightly in mine as the taxi winds uphill along the modern roads that lead to the Albaicin's medieval labyrinth of steep cobblestoned streets. I make idle conversation with the driver whilst mentally taking stock of where I am. The roads may be paved in concrete now, and have traffic lights and roundabouts, but I still remember every inch as if I were once again riding them on horseback. It is the strange layering of time that all immortals must endure, the memory of a place as it once was lying beneath modernity like a trick of the shadows. When the taxi stops at the point where the road gives way to the Albaicin's cobblestoned steps, we step out, and the air hits me like a shock from those long-gone times, the scents assailing my senses in a rush of memory that is almost painful.

Citron and jasmine. Fresh mint and sugar. The dankness of old plumbing cut through by exotic scents of a thousand types of tea, which I recall being sold in a nearby open market. Rather more disturbingly, the air is redolent with the vague scent of frankincense, which Granadinos famously burn in braziers on many street corners.

Vampires have always made Granada their home, alongside an array of witches, wolves, and other supernatural creatures. The frankincense might be thought a quirk of a very Catholic country or an old superstition by the tourists. The Granadinos, however, know exactly why they burn it. Gypsies, or *gitanos*, as the Spanish call them, have been living in the caves of the hills bordering the Albaicin since the 15th century, and know well what monsters and magic lurk in the stone alleyways. They also know that frankincense keeps a specific type of monster at bay: vampires like Harper and me.

Of all the damned places, I think, with a sudden, impatient fury, *why must the girls be so determined to call Granada home?* Knowing the answer to my rhetorical question does nothing to improve my mood.

"Antoine." It takes a moment before I realize I'm clutching Harper's hand hard enough to make her wince and notice the concern in her voice. "Antoine. Are you alright? Do we need to take a moment before we walk down to the house?"

I suck in my breath and try to steady my voice. "Perhaps," I say tightly. "Perhaps a moment."

We sit at a small table in a sunlit plaza and order red wine. It comes with the free tapas for which Granada is famous. I push calamari around the plate without tasting it. I have no appetite for the wine, the food, or even, somewhat unusually, for blood.

I remember too much blood in this place to desire more.

"You know they aren't going to give up." Harper is staring at me with an unusually grim expression. "The girls have been pushing us for information about the events surrounding their birth, and about Callie and Jeremiah, since they were old enough to verbalize the questions. We've tried to manage it by telling them as little as we can, or by heading them off. But given that they have now been living in Granada for four years, and clearly have no intention of leaving, I think we can safely say our efforts have failed."

"What are you suggesting?" I turn the glass slowly in one hand, holding her eyes. "That we just tell them all we know? Do you honestly think they will simply let it lie?"

"Do you think they have been letting it lie so far?" Harper raises her eyebrows. "Antoine, we left France because the twins wouldn't stop trying to find a way back to Revolutionary Paris. We left Italy after you discovered that when Aurelia wasn't busy training with 16th century fencing masters, she was trying to unlock the waterpaths leading back to Napoleonic Italy. The one place you flatly refused to bring them was to Spain—and they made a beeline for it the moment they left home.

"The only reason they've not actually gone back to the Napoleonic wars is because through some twist of fate, the waterpaths leading to that era won't open for them. But you and I don't fully understand exactly what the girls can and can't do, because we've always avoided talking about any of it. Maybe it's time we changed tactics."

My throat begins to close over, unreasoning anger rising inside me. Long before I met Harper, I thought I'd mastered that anger, gained control over myself and emotions.

But here is what I have learned: self-mastery is a fragile thing, undone as soon as I face the prospect of my wife or daughters in danger. Then, my control is blown to the winds, and a wild, terrifying fury takes hold of me, born of fear and the knowledge that no matter how I try, I cannot control the vagaries of fate. I try not to let that fear show, and I believe I can say I have never allowed the fury to impact my family. But that does not mean they are unaware of its existence, and even that weakness infuriates me.

I take a deep breath and force my voice to remain calm. "Then I take it you think it's time we told them the truth about the role Guidry played, and about their connection to Avery through their blood?"

"I don't think we have any choice, Antoine." Harper's eyes on mine are understanding, but resolute, nonetheless. "I think it's time we told our daughters everything we know about what happened when they were born—and about why we don't want them to search for answers."

CHAPTER 2

TWINS

Antoine

It's late afternoon when we knock on the heavy wooden door to our daughters' carmen. Set into a whitewashed wall, it has a smaller door cut into it, leaving a high beam of wood to step over that once served as an obstacle to men with swords in their hands. The days when every house might need to serve as a fortress for its inhabitants are not so much historical trivia for me, but painful memory.

The courtyard within is even more beautiful than during Harper's and my last visit a year ago. Pomegranate trees hang over the walls, and citron trees flourish in terracotta pots. The white mosaic paving is inlaid with a design of flower filled urns. Jasmine crawls along the walls, and a large, ancient fig grows in one corner. Water, so revered and understood by the Moors who built the Albaicin, trickles from several fountains.

"Darling!" Harper has caught Marguerite in her arms, her own flaming hair indistinguishable from that of the younger of our twins. Aurelia hangs back, eyeing the embracing pair with a guarded expression.

"Dad," she acknowledges me quietly. She leads the way inside without waiting for her mother's embrace, and my heart constricts at Harper's brief expression of hurt. But Harper knows as well as I not to push Aurelia for shows of affection. Our eldest daughter might have been born only moments before Marguerite, and share with uncanny precision her sister's features, but there the similarity ends. If Marguerite has inherited her mother's artistic nature as well as Harper's flaming hair and emerald eyes, along with Aurelia's dark Marigny coloring has come my own ability to shutter her emotions behind flat, cobalt eyes.

If there is such a thing as karma, Aurelia has delivered it to me—with interest.

I follow her through a second door, to the internal courtyard, the center piece of which is a fragrant herb garden that I imagine is Marguerite's doing. She has inherited Harper's green thumb, and a dose, I suspect, of her mother's magical ability to coax even the most stubborn plant to grow.

Hanging on a rear wall is evidence of Aurelia's rather different talents: several swords dating from various eras; various crossbows; as well as a gun cabinet, a myriad of knives, and an array of other weapons designed to deliver death. Aurelia catches me staring at them, and her mouth quirks slightly at the edges. She raises her eyebrows at me challengingly. I take yet another deep breath and plaster a smile on my face.

Parenthood.

"Connor and Cass will arrive with the others," Marguerite chatters on cheerfully as she hugs me. "They're in Brazil, I think, or maybe it's Argentina now? I'm not sure. Cass's group moves around a lot." Cass is a vampire, married to Harper's brother Connor, who can shift into wolf form. Thanks to me, he is also immortal, yet another example of the mysterious effects of my blood. Cass is a musician, and for the past decade she's played with a Spanish group from Granada who just happen to also be vampires. They move around a lot, especially given that the group have called Granada home since the days of Arabic rule and are positively allergic to publicity of any kind. I'm not sorry they are absent for another day or so. If I'm entirely honest, I've never really forgiven Cass and Connor for giving the girls a home in the one damned city I hoped they'd never visit.

I catch Aurelia smirking at me, and hastily compose my features. My eldest daughter has an uncanny ability to read my mind. "I'm glad they can make it." I fake a smile. "It will be nice to see them again."

Marguerite and Harper take my remark on face value and continue to chatter. Aurelia's smirk just deepens. She folds her arms and leans against the wall, staring at me with barely disguised amusement as Marguerite busies herself making us all tea.

Tea, I think resignedly, longing for the very good whiskey I have sitting on the shelf in England. My eyes catch Aurelia's, and her own flicker briefly toward the terrace. "I'm just taking Dad up to see my new crossbow," she says quietly, and Marguerite waves her away, though Harper, I notice, gives us both a rather narrow glance.

Very little escapes my wife.

I follow Aurelia up the narrow staircase and come out onto the terracotta terrace, half of which is covered by a wooden pergola dripping with purple wisteria that will offer welcome shade in a few months, at the height of a blazing Spanish summer. The other half is open, and affords a magnificent view straight across the valley, to the curved turrets and arched windows of the Alhambra.

Aurelia reaches behind a potted orange tree for a bottle which she brandishes triumphantly. "It's Spanish single malt," she says, pouring two glasses. "Made with water from the Sierra Nevada and aged in sherry barrels from Jerez." She raises her glass and fixes me with a challenging eye. *"Por Espana me atrevo,"* she murmurs, holding my eyes as she drinks.

For Spain, I dare. The motto of her regiment, which just happens to have its origins in the guerrillero fighters who long ago fought against Napoleon's occupation of Spain. I'm not naïve enough to think Aurelia's choice was some kind of coincidence. The toast is yet another a reminder of the life she has chosen, one I would never have wished upon her.

Mastering my features with no small effort, I raise my own glass, though I can't bring myself to echo the toast.

The whiskey has a spicy nuttiness to it that isn't unpleasant at all, and a crisp finish that feels like the pure mountain water from which it is made. "Not bad," I say, holding the glass up to the falling sun. "Not bad at all."

We stand in silence for a moment, watching the earthen walls of the ancient palaces opposite turn umber in the late afternoon sun. The Albaicin is full of sounds from another life: donkey's hooves clattering along the cobblestones; birdsong; the haunting strains of a street performer playing flamenco. No cars drive through these narrow alleyways. To me, who has experienced Granada across the centuries, life here feels in some ways as it always has, blurring the line between past and present even more profoundly.

I inhale sharply, trying to shake the disorienting feeling, and turn to Aurelia. "When did you get back from Mali?" I realize my mistake as soon as the words are out of my mouth.

"Amazing that you should know I was there, given that our mission was top secret information." Aurelia's tone is dry, though, rather than hostile, and when I chance a look, she is half smiling, and shaking her head. "I suppose I should be grateful that you didn't come out there and spy on me."

I did, actually. But I'm hardly about to share that piece of information with her.

"I got back a week ago," she answers my question. "And I have a month of leave after today."

"A month." I nod as if I hadn't hacked into her roster weeks ago, trying to think of how to phrase my next question. "Are you planning to . . .go anywhere? Spend some time with someone special, maybe?"

"Oh, Dad." She rolls her eyes. "You're about as subtle as a sledgehammer. If you're asking if I have a boyfriend, the answer is no, unless you count an entire squadron of stinking boys who barely notice I'm a woman. And if by 'go anywhere' you're asking whether I plan to travel into the past on my time off, the answer is definitely no." She meets my eyes with a certain hardness in her own. "I have enough trouble in my own life without chasing my sister when she finds her way into more."

I want to ask what she means, but know she is unlikely to give me more information. I know that Marguerite falls into the waterpaths more easily than Aurelia. Know, too, that one of the reasons my eldest daughter begged me to train her in martial arts at a young age was so she knew how to defend them both, if Marguerite's travels led them into danger. I didn't want to train her; what father wants to admit they can't protect their own children? But the first time the twins returned from their water path travels covered in blood, I changed my mind pretty quickly. At first, reluctant to worry Harper more than she already was, I trained Aurelia in secret. It scared me how fast my daughter learned. Given her rapid improvement, she was clearly using the skills regularly in her secret travels. When Harper found out what we were doing, it caused one of the biggest arguments of all time in our marriage—until I explained the reasons why.

We never argued about me training Aurelia again, and soon after, Harper began spending a lot of time teaching Marguerite herb lore, and how to use plant medicines. I guess both of us have done what we can, however inadequate that might feel, to help our children survive in times and places which, for the most part, we can only imagine.

"And your sister?" I clear my throat, unsure how to ask what I want to know. If Aurelia is stubborn and unreadable, Marguerite is elusive as the water paths into which she falls. Getting a straight answer from either of them is like extracting blood from a stone. "Is she still . . .traveling?"

"Not if I have anything to do with it." Aurelia's answer is so abrupt that I turn, slightly taken aback by the hard light in her eyes.

"Are you two arguing, then?"

"Not exactly." Aurelia shrugs, a curt gesture that is so terribly like my own that I instantly recognize the pain it masks. "Let's just say that I see little point in chasing after whispers from voices that died centuries ago, or choosing love affairs that are doomed to end in flowers on a gravestone."

Her eyes are dark slate with heartache I wasn't there to fix, and shadows of experiences I can never understand. The bleakness of her words, and the picture they paint, shame me into silence.

"I've had enough of living in the past, Dad. And Marguerite won't travel unless I go with her. So, you find us in something of a cold war, this visit." She raises her glass to me again, this time in an ironic gesture that doesn't lessen the pain I sense behind it. "Happy birthday to us, hey Dad?"

This time when we drink, I put my hand on her shoulder, and after a moment, she lays her head on it. We stand there quietly, watching night fall over the valley, until the sun has gone, and amber night lights have turned the Alhambra walls ochre.

CHAPTER 3

LOVE

Harper

"I've been taking tour groups through the Alhambra." Marguerite lifts the kettle from the stove and pours it into an Arabic style silver teapot. "I really enjoy spending time there. The Nasrid palaces are so beautiful." Hearing the almost wistful note in her voice makes me smile. My youngest daughter takes the same pleasure in the aesthetics of her surroundings that I always have, and it gives me a sense of quiet happiness to see the herbs growing on the windowsill, and the filigree glasses into which she has placed fresh mint in preparation for the tea.

Aurelia, much like her father, rarely seems to notice her surroundings at all, unless it is to gauge what risks might exist within it. She also shares Antoine's reluctance to 'worry' me by telling me about those risks. Antoine can protest all he likes that Aurelia doesn't confide in him, either, but part of me knows she trusts him in a way she doesn't me. Antoine also insists that Marguerite confides in me, rather than him, but the truth is, whilst my younger daughter may resemble me in appearance and, to some degree, in nature, she is as much a closed book to me as her sister.

"I'm glad you enjoy taking the tours." I smile at Marguerite. "And that you're doing something that gives you a break from the university. You seem to be working very hard, lately." I try not to make the remark a question. The truth is that even thinking about Marguerite's work makes me feel mildly sick. Marguerite was barely two years old when Antoine and I realized how easily she fell into the waterpaths. By the time the girls were five, we understood that unlike Aurelia, Marguerite had little control over her travels back in time. That was when we made the twins promise that they would never travel without the other. Since Aurelia has joined the army, however, I can't stop imagining Marguerite falling down the pathways, with nobody to follow her there.

"I've been running a course of lectures on the Court of Lions, in the Alhambra," she says, her face turned away from me so I can't read her expression. "It's the same part of the palaces I focused my dissertation on." There's a studied casualness in her words that gives me a prickle of unease.

"Oh?" I say, trying my best to sound politely interested rather than inquisitive. I know all too well how fast my girls shut down if they suspect I am probing for information.

"For such a famous part of the palaces, very little is known about the fountain at the center of that courtyard," Marguerite explains, turning back to me. The afternoon sunlight catches her eyes, turning them a deep, glittering emerald that makes my breath catch. Sometimes she reminds me almost unbearably of Tessa, my own, long dead twin sister. It is poignant to catch those glimpses, just as it is to see fleeting echoes of Jeremiah in Aurelia's solemn eyes. It might be the girls who travel pathways to the past, but sometimes it feels as if the past lives all around us, in those I love, and here, in the very air I breathe. Just knowing that Jeremiah and Callie once inhabited this house gives me the same bittersweet longing I feel when I see Tessa's expression in my daughter's eyes.

"Much of what we know about the fountain can only be speculation," Marguerite continues. "It is immensely frustrating." She frowns, and I stifle a smile. Different as they might be in nature, in some things, Aurelia and Marguerite are entirely the same. Neither of them is remotely able to let a problem go unsolved.

"And that isn't something you have tried to . . .deduce?" I ask carefully.

Marguerite casts me a look that is the closest she gets to rolling her eyes. "Obviously, if traveling back in time would answer my questions, I'd go," she says, rather impatiently. "But the historical facts around the fountain that remain a mystery lie down waterpaths that are closed to me."

"Really?" I lean forward, intrigued. This is new information to me. "I thought it was only the one era you couldn't access?"

"Well, some of the fountain restorations were made during the Napoleonic wars, which have always been closed to us." She frowns at the teapot, turning the glass in her hand. "But I've found most of the waterpaths leading to the construction of the Court of Lions and its fountain closed to me." She shoots me a rather guilty smile. "To be honest, that's why I did my dissertation on that part of the Alhambra. It was one of the only areas I had to study to understand, rather than simply visit."

I shake my head in mock remonstration, although I can't help but laugh with her. There are humorous aspects to the girls' ability, even if the dangers posed by time travel have given me more sleepless nights than any parent should have to endure. "But I thought you told us you had travelled back to much of the early construction of the palaces?"

"Oh, I did. I do." Marguerite nods readily. "Usually, I can ask to be shown the details of any building, and the waterpaths will take me back to the specific moment that explains it. But when it comes to the Court of Lions, I have asked direct questions—like what the poet, Ibn Zamrak, meant exactly by the words he had carved on the bowl of the fountain. But no matter how much I've touched the words, and held the thought in my mind, I cannot so much as catch sight of the man. It's quite maddening, if I'm honest." She looks up at me and grins rather wickedly. "But I did meet some girls from the Emir's harem, who told me poems of a far more interesting nature."

It's my turn to roll my eyes, though again, she makes me laugh. Both girls tend to be reasonably straightforward about the travels in the waterpaths they have done for professional, or fact finding, reasons.

It's the other stories they don't tell us. Like the year they were twelve, when we spent a week in Chattanooga, Tennessee, so we could hike some of the Appalachian trail. It was several days before Antoine and I had realized that the girls' pale faces and insatiable thirst had nothing to do with the hard miles they were hiking each day, and everything to do with their daily adventures into the waterpaths. The growth spurts in the latter part of the week were truly alarming and pointed to the girls having spent months at a time in the past, something neither Antoine nor I could ever be certain of, given the girls' ability to return to a precise moment. We had become accustomed to their seeming far more mature than others their age, but back then, we hadn't realized just how often they were traveling, how much time they spent in the waterpaths. It was only when we visited the Chickamauga civil war battlefield, and Marguerite fell to the ground, sobbing in terrible, heartbroken cries, that the story had come tumbling out. To witness a child's first broken heart is one thing. To learn the twins had spent months visiting one of the bloodiest and most dangerous sites of the entire civil war, and both fallen in love with soldiers who had later died in the conflict, had been utterly horrifying. Though perhaps it had been even harder to realize that for every day we lived together, our girls likely lived another, somewhere in a time we couldn't share.

I learned later that after that summer, Aurelia had sworn never to fall in love with a man in the past again.

Marguerite, however, is a different story. Although she is more forthcoming about her love life than Aurelia, she, too, has her secrets. Given some of the stories she has shared with me, that's not necessarily a bad thing. Discovering one's daughter spent a summer being Picasso's lover is something most mothers would, I suspect, prefer not to hear.

"Are you—seeing anyone, then?" I ask cautiously.

Marguerite's face falls. "No."

Rather taken aback by her abrupt dismissal, I wait, unsure what to say. Eventually Marguerite looks sideways at me and heaves a rather dramatic sigh.

"You're not going to let that go, are you," she says resignedly.

I shrug. *I'm a mother. Of course, I'm not going to let it go.*

Marguerite turns the glass in front of her slowly, the tea swirling around the mint leaves within it. "Aurelia won't let me travel anymore." The way she says it sets alarm bells off, but I remain quiet. "Or that is, she won't let me travel unless it's for work purposes. And even then, I must make it quick. No more long visits. And no more . . . entanglements." She doesn't need to specify what she means. But it isn't the reference to her stalled love life that concerns me.

"No more long visits?" I try not to sound worried. "Why is that?" I want to ask her just how long some of those visits have been, but I can't. It terrifies me to think that the girls may be using a finite number of mortal years on this earth to travel into the past, rather than spending them with us. And no matter how selfish I know that sounds, I can't help it. Every day I am away from them I fear I'm wasting a day of what might well be very short lives, especially in comparison to my own eternity, which I can't bear to contemplate without my daughters in it.

But Marguerite appears unaware of my consternation. She's frowning at the table, clearly unhappy. "Aurelia thinks we should try to live our lives in this time. She says there's no future for us in the past, that we need to try to make lives for ourselves in this one."

Despite Marguerite's abrupt tone and clear disapproval of this plan, I find myself silently thanking my eldest daughter. "Perhaps your sister has a point," I begin tentatively, but in a rare display of anger, Marguerite cuts me off.

"No. She doesn't. Aurelia is just scared, that's all. But just because she doesn't want to fall in love in the past again, it shouldn't mean I can't—or that she gets to dictate where and when we can travel." At the sound of footsteps descending from the terrace, Marguerite stops speaking, and shoots me a warning glance.

I compose my face into a neutral expression, and bite back the thousand questions on my lips.

CHAPTER 4

SECRETS

Harper

We eat on the terrace, the Alhambra glowing russet on the opposite side of the valley. A waxing moon rises over the palaces, lighting the snowcapped mountains so they appear to float on an indigo sky. From a nearby bar, the haunting strains of *cante jondo*, the 'deep song' of flamenco, carries to us on fragrant evening air.

"Beautiful," I say softly.

"Uh huh," Aurelia says around a mouthful of rucola and partisan salad. "Sure beats army cooking."

Marguerite shakes her head, but she's smiling, and it touches my heart. "Which is why I cook when you're home," she says. "Not all of us consider MRE's to be actual food."

Antoine catches my eye, and I see in his expression the same mix of wonder and joy that I feel in these moments, in the odd bliss of domesticity. Small pleasures that neither of us will ever take for granted, not least because of the ever-present fear that such moments are fragile, so easily lost to us forever. I shiver despite the mild night, and a shadow falls over Antoine's eyes.

He feels it too, the fragility of this life. The unending, corrosive terror that it will all disappear, our girls gone forever, whether lost in the water paths, or taken by a life we fear they may not be built to survive.

"I'm taking a group of students to the Alhambra tomorrow." Marguerite is looking down at her plate, so I can't see her eyes. "I thought you all might like to join me, see what I've been working on." Her voice is casual enough, but given Antoine's past, there's inherent tension in the question. I notice it isn't only Antoine who stiffens, but Aurelia too.

Interesting.

"I'm not sure—" Antoine demurs.

"I've got a lot on," Aurelia says at the same time.

There's a slight pause, filled with all the things we don't discuss. I wait a beat, then say firmly, "Well, I'd love to go, darling. I think a family day out sounds wonderful." I don't directly challenge the other two, but their visible squirming is amusing to watch.

Antoine cracks first. "Well, if you want to go," he says reluctantly. Then, seeing Marguerite's rather crestfallen expression, he hurries on. "Of course, I'd love to see you work, sweetheart. It's just . . .been a long time, since I've visited the Alhambra."

Aurelia's eyes narrow, and Marguerite's gleam with sharp interest, but neither of them ask a direct question. They both know better than to ask their father about the past, especially about his time in Granada. It's all part of the silence we have both kept in relation to Jeremiah and Callie, or about anything about a past we both suspect holds dangers even worse than those posed by human conflict.

The same past we need to tell them about.

But not yet, I think. *Please, let us just have a day. One day.*

It's Aurelia's reaction, though, that really intrigues me. My eldest daughter is now staring at her sister accusingly, whilst Marguerite is studiously avoiding her eyes. By the expression in

Aurelia's, I take it that Marguerite has just manipulated her into doing something she had already refused.

"A tour of the Alhambra," she says flatly, confirming my suspicions. "Do you really think that's a good use of our time, Marguerite?" There's just enough emphasis on the word 'time' to set my nerves on edge.

"I think that ignoring a building many consider to be the eighth wonder of the world would be a pity." Marguerite's tone is determinedly light, but Aurelia audibly huffs. Antoine's eyes narrow in an expression uncannily reminiscent of Aurelia a moment ago. His eyes flicker to mine, and I can read the question in them: *is now the time?*

But despite our earlier agreement to disclose all we know of the past, and the girls' story, I can't help wanting to hold on to this moment, for the one day I've promised myself, at least. I have a feeling that after we speak, the atmosphere on this terrace may not be quite so relaxed. I shake my head almost imperceptibly, and Antoine lifts his chin in silent acknowledgment. He turns to ask Marguerite about her work, and the awkward moment passes.

Secrets. I sigh inwardly. I'm so tired of them. At the same time, I'm horribly aware that once they are spoken, any trace of peace may well be noticeably absent for a time.

"When are the others arriving for this party, anyway?" Aurelia fixes me with a direct stare so like her father's that it makes my heart twist. She doesn't mention any guests of her own, and I feel the customary mixture of guilt and sadness at the strange life our daughters are forced to live, never able to truly disclose who they are, outside our own small supernatural circle.

"Tomorrow night," I say. "Cass and Connor need to keep a low profile. Tate and Iara are traveling from Venezuela. They will all arrive late, after darkness falls." I say the last line unthinkingly, but it's too late. A shadow crosses Aurelia's eyes, turning the fathomless cobalt to dark slate, and I curse myself for reminding her that even something so simple as a family birthday gathering must require secrecy and stealth. But Cass and Connor lived here in Granada for over a decade. Their faces are well known, and like Antoine and I in Deepwater Hollow, their lack of ageing became awkward to explain. Tate was also lecturing here at the university for a couple of years. It's better if they all maintain a low profile to avoid being recognized. I wanted to hold the celebrations in England, or even France, for just this reason, but the girls insisted we have it here. I suspect they plan to use the opportunity of having us all together, in Granada no less, to ask some hard questions of their own. It's one of the reasons I've been trying to prepare Antoine to have conversations I know he would rather avoid.

We never really meant to hide the twins' story from them. At first, topics like the loss of Jeremiah and Callie, and the mysterious disappearance of Guidry, Antoine's oldest friend, were simply too painful to speak of.

Avery, my old friend who used some of Antoine and my blood to transform herself into an immortal creature that even I don't truly understand, left Deepwater Hollow and never came back. She promised us back then that she would never harm the twins, and over twenty years later, I have no reason to think she lied. Given how many challenges the girls face, it has seemed unnecessarily cruel to raise specters of the past that can only cause them more pain.

But at some point, all those topics got bound up together into a great ball of silence. And over the past few years, as the girls have settled tentatively into the first stability they have ever really known since childhood, that ball of silence has grown to loom across our relationship like a storm waiting to break. And not just over our small family of four. I know that Tate, Iara, Connor and Cass have kept their distance from us in recent years not least because they dislike keeping our secrets.

Connor has accused me more than once of doing the girls a disservice by not disclosing all we know. My brother has never been one for hiding his opinions—or the truth, no matter how awkward.

"Are you inviting any of your own friends?" I ask, to shake off my own dark thoughts. Aurelia's slightly incredulous expression makes me instantly regret my words.

"It would be a little hard to explain, don't you think?" Her mouth curls rather contemptuously. "Quite apart from having to lie about our age, we'd have to explain who you all are. And that many supes in the same room . . ." Her voice trails off, and she lifts a shoulder in silent comment.

She's right, of course. One supernatural creature might occasion no more than the odd glance. Two, even. But six immortals, with our chiseled features, strange iridescent eyes, and elongated forms, make a rather dramatic picture. And Antoine isn't great at pretending he's not a father, just as I find it difficult to pretend I'm merely a close friend or relative.

"Anyway." Aurelia casts me a slightly challenging look. "I'm looking forward to having the whole family together again. Being able to talk openly." She holds my eyes just long enough to make her point, and I sigh inwardly.

It looks like Antoine and I are having that conversation, whether we are ready, or not.

CHAPTER 5

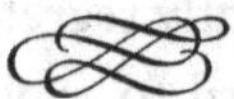

DREAMS

Aurelia

I'm dreaming of the Alhambra, and the fountain is whispering to me again.

In my dream it is nighttime, moonbeams shining down on the pale marble floor. At the center of the Court of Lions the fountain is running, but not with water.

It's running with blood.

I can't hear what the whispers are saying. I never can when they come from the waterpaths that lead to the past. Instead, I feel them, emotional cords that pull me back in time with the promise of adventure, or the intrigue of mystery. But this cord is different.

It is desire.

Desire so primal it leaves me aching with longing, helpless to resist the fountain's magnetic pull. The water is roiling, blood red shot through with a strange seam of gold that both fascinates and repels me at once. It gives off a wild, intoxicating scent, like fir and pine high in the mountains. The scent feels exhilarating and terrifying at once, stealing into my being like a dangerous drug, threatening the heart I have sworn never to lose again in the waterpaths.

The blood-filled pendant I wear about my neck is gleaming with strange, electrical flashes like a distant storm, the pulsating vial a searing heat against my skin. Every instinct warns me to run. But my body is on fire, my logical mind dulled, and I am inexorably drawn toward the blood red water. My feet scrabble for purchase on the smooth marble. The pendant is tugging me forward, but I know I must fight the pull.

No matter how much I want to fall into the waterpaths, I know I cannot. *It isn't safe.*

"Aurelia!"

In my dream, Marguerite, my twin, is on the other side of the fountain. Her pendant is equally turbulent and her voice is shrill with fear. I realize in horror that her pendant is rising from her chest, pulling her toward the fountain. Her form is shimmering, beginning to ripple as it does when she falls into the waterpaths. Marguerite has never been able to control the fall like I can. Whatever force is tugging at me is pulling her, also, and she isn't strong enough to resist.

"Aurelia!" This time when she calls me her voice is tired, desperate, and I know she cannot fight anymore. My fear breaks through the strange haze holding me. I lunge for her across the blood red water.

I wake abruptly, covered in sweat, my heart thudding like a drum. The pendant at my neck pulses like a living thing. Its heat matches the dull, aching pulse between my legs. I stifle a groan of sadness, the longing of unmet desire. Not knowing what, or who, it is I am longing for, only makes the feeling worse.

But you will not go in search of answers, I tell myself fiercely. I know that following those whispers is impossible. I know the dangers of following my heart into the waterpaths. *I will not chase love that can only end in flowers on a gravestone.*

"Aurelia." I turn, startled, to find Marguerite staring at me from her bed on the other side of the room. The Spanish moon shines through our open window, turning my sister's auburn curls to pale flame. Although our features are entirely identical, our coloring is completely different. My black curls and cobalt eyes are my father's Marigny coloring. Marguerite's fiery hair and deep emerald eyes are identical to those of our mother. We take after our respective parents in other ways, too. Marguerite has Mom's artistic nature, and green thumb.

I have my father's natural affinity with deadly weapons.

We do, however, have one important thing in common: a shared lifetime of traveling the mysterious waterpaths into the past.

"Another dream?" She holds out her hand across the tiled floor. I nod wordlessly, taking comfort from the solid physicality of her touch. Her eyes drop to the pendant at my neck. The blood in it swirls, still gleaming with mercurial light. Marguerite's pendant is equally turbulent, though the light in hers seems silver rather than gold. She squeezes my hand. "We have to talk about it, Aurelia."

I am saved from answering by a soft thud on the terrace above. I put my free finger to my lips, but the warning is unnecessary. We learned the art of silent communication at an early age. Our parents are vampires, gifted with supernatural hearing, among other talents. They are currently staying in the room above us, and have clearly just returned from hunting.

Marguerite and I close our eyes and feign sleep, though our hands remain clasped. I'm not ready to let go of my sister just yet. My dream is still too fresh, the terror of losing her too real. I've been following Marguerite down the waterpaths our entire lives. It's one of the reasons I wound up in the Spanish Special Forces. The past isn't always a safe place, and Marguerite has a knack for finding trouble. One of us had to learn early how to fight.

Our parents push the door open softly and peek in at us.

"Look at them." Mom's whisper is full of love. I don't have to open my eyes to know hers are glistening, nor that Dad's grim features are temporarily softened, his hand holding hers. Dad had been a vampire for three centuries when he met Mom. Unbeknown to them both, her blood contained powers of earth magic that not only saved Dad's life when he was drained to death, but also temporarily made him human, which is how we were conceived.

They watch us for a few more moments before I hear them leave. They've done this since we were small, come in to see us after they've been hunting, watching over us to ensure their miracle babies are safe.

"They love each other so much." Marguerite's whisper is filled with longing.

"Too much, perhaps." I know my response sounds harsh. But if Marguerite craves a love like that shared by our parents, one so all-consuming both would willingly die rather than lose the other, I find even the thought of such vulnerability terrifying. The sensations from my dream rush over me in a hot wave that momentarily steals my breath and makes my body limp, as if underscoring the point. I shiver, withdrawing my hand from Marguerite's, but her eyes narrow, and I know it's too late. My sister and I live in one another's dreams, just as we travel the chaos of the waterpaths in unconscious partnership. We are linked not only by our pendants and the blood in our veins, but on some other plane that transcends the physical. Marguerite might not know what I felt in the dream, but she was unmistakably there, and had her own experience of it.

"We must talk about it, Aurelia. The Alhambra, and the fountain. It's a gateway to the closed paths—"

"I know that." Even in the barely audible whisper we mastered as children, my tone is abrupt as I cut her off. "I know we do. Just not right now. Not after that dream." I take her hand again and squeeze it in apology, trying to take the sting from my words.

After a moment, her eyes soften. "Okay." She returns the pressure on my hand. "But soon."

She watches me until I nod silently, then I hear her breath change as she drifts off to sleep. Her hand remains in mine, a silent bond that nobody else can understand, and which comforts me more than I might like to admit. In a world where everything from our mortality to the contents of our pendants is unknown, only Marguerite and I know the life we have shared, the terror and exhilaration of the waterpaths. It's a bond that usually transcends our personal differences. *Until that damned fountain.*

I roll over and will myself back to sleep, trying to ignore the heat still pulsing through my body. It seems to me that the intoxicating scent of pine and fir still lingers on the air. The seductive promise of that scent is terrifying enough, but it is the other presence I sense that terrifies me.

There is a darkness in that fountain. I know it, as surely as I know I should run as far as I can from the wild scent that has begun to feel like an invisible cord tugging me toward the abyss of emotion and desire I've spent years trying to avoid. The darkness is a different presence. Predatory. An insidious shadow lurking within the chaos of the waterpaths, waiting for the right moment to strike.

The truth is that dream is not the first time I've smelled that scent, nor felt that shadow of danger. But the waterpaths are a chaotic space, amid which all is confusion. Before Marguerite took me to visit the fountain in the Alhambra's Court of Lions, the scent was no more than a haunting siren call on the periphery of my consciousness, whilst the predatory shadow was a ghost gone with the dawn.

But there was nothing vague about the visceral, shattering pull I felt standing by that fountain. And since then, the dreams have become a nightly torture, and the cord an ever-present pressure tugging me toward what feels like a precipice.

I have never considered myself a coward. But the abyss of emotion and desire beyond that precipice terrifies me more than any theater of war ever has. And the predatory shadow feels as enveloping as the deep cold of coming snow.

And yet despite my fears, I fall asleep half wishing to find that scent again, almost reaching for the precipice. In my dreams the abyss reaches toward me, a swirling darkness full of emotion I both crave, and do not dare trust.

CHAPTER 6

GHOSTS

Antoine

I wait until my three girls are all asleep before I slip from the Albaicin house into the shadowed alleyways.

I can't visit the Alhambra for the first time in over two hundred years in the company of my daughters, or even my wife. This is something I must do alone, a demon I need to face without witnesses.

I race silently down to the stone bridge crossing the Darro River and continue up the ancient road on the northern side of the palace walls. Water rushes down the hill in a narrow canal between myself and the Alhambra walls. Trees overhang the road, their boughs heavy with leaves. I remember when the trees were saplings, and the palaces were a fortress held by the French.

I remember it all too well.

I leap silently over the southeast wall, landing amid fragrant plants and rushing water. The secrets of irrigation and horticulture were a gift the Moorish conquerors brought to Spain, and nowhere did their skills reach more transcendent heights than on the grounds of the Alhambra. I never walked these gardens, however, marveling at the exquisite flowers and water features. I heard others exclaim over them. The air carried their voices eight meters below ground, down to where I lay, chained and bleeding.

I stalk grimly through the fragrant paradise, heedless of the beauty around me. I'm here for one purpose only: to face the demons of memory.

I had feared that years and the Alhambra restorations may make it harder for me to find my way to the dungeon in which I was kept.

They don't.

Sooner than I'm ready for, I'm standing by an aqueduct that carries water to the palaces, staring at the crumbling remains of towers that were still intact on the night I was captured and brought here. I last saw them the day I escaped, but the ruins that remain bear no resemblance to the towers I remember. They wouldn't, of course. The French did their best to blow the entire Alhambra to hell that day. Had I not escaped, I might well have gone with it.

Even the crumbling remains of those towers send a chill through my entire body. I last saw their outline through a blood and pain filled haze.

I follow the pathways more hesitantly as I come closer to the circular hole in the ground that marks the dungeon in which I was held. My breath comes short, the yawning pit beckoning me like a dark seductress. It's a strange experience for a vampire, to be short of breath. But in this place, more than any other, my immortality afforded me no protection. I thought I would die here. I very nearly did. Even now, the memory of my imprisonment and torture is palpable, a heaviness in the air that feels as real to me as any of the stone remains. Standing at the edge of that terrible pit, past and present entwine about me like the chains in which I was held. At any moment I expect to see my old nemesis, the French Lieutenant Arkady Dumont. To hear his hard accents shrieking manically on the night, "Tell me what you know!"

I force myself to step forward, and stare down into the darkness.

The opening is about twelve yards in diameter. Even now, I can recall staring up at the light from inside the hole, every stone at the edge of it imprinted on my memory. I had been shackled tightly in chains impregnated with frankincense, and lowered into a pit where more was burning, the acrid stench of it searing my insides with every breath until I was mad with the pain.

Arkady Dumont had known exactly what I was. Known, and suspected me of being even more.

Because centuries before they were born, and long before I had any idea of the true magic in my blood, Arkady Dumont had known about my daughters.

I take a deep breath and leap into the pit.

The smell assails me as soon as I land, and it's only by sheer effort of will that I do not instinctively retch at the sensations it brings.

Helplessness. A terrible, dark, corrosive thirst, made worse by the prisoners bound and bleeding nearby, men beside whom I have fought and who now I must fight myself not to kill out of desperation . . .

Horrific despair, born of bewilderment and terrible, brutal pain. I would have answered Arkady's questions, if I could have. God knows I wanted to. I'd have done anything to be gone from this place. But in the game we played, Arkady understood more than I, and the answers he sought were mysteries I could not fathom.

Until two hundred years later, when my daughters were born, and finally, his questions began to make sense.

I clench my fists and force myself to breathe deeply, inhaling the air in a steady rhythm. Tomorrow I must stand beside this pit and listen to Marguerite talk to her students about the poor prisoners who were captive here. Harper will be watching me closely, for although she knows the bare facts of my imprisonment, even she doesn't know the truth of what happened here. Before the birth of our daughters, my imprisonment here was part of a distant past I had long tried to forget. After their birth, and Guidry's disappearance, the implications of my time here have been so terrifying that I haven't wanted to burden her with my suspicions. And when I discovered the water paths to the Napoleonic era were closed to the twins, I thought that perhaps Arkady had been mistaken, or misled.

Even now, I cling to the hope that my daughters never come anywhere near this place, during that time.

But some other part of me knows my wishes are in vain. And that means I must tell the girls my own story. Which is why I came here tonight.

I needed to face this place, and these memories, alone. Master myself before I attempt to explain what I know. Which is little enough, in the end, and raises more questions than it does provide answers.

I stand still in the dank silence, forcing myself to sit amid the discomfort and breathe in the memories and sensations, then release them on an exhalation. It is a technique I learned under a Japanese master more than a century and a half ago, when the nightmares of my time here could still wake me in a screaming, sweating mess that no amount of blood or whiskey could drive away.

My breathing slows, and gradually I feel the air around me become just air, the fear leached from it, the specters held in my memory no longer real.

When at last my pulse is steady and my body relaxed, I leap to the surface, the action itself a profound reminder of the difference between this time and that. To have lain there, knowing salvation was no more than a leap away, yet entirely unable to move so much as a muscle for the screaming, burning agony of my frankincense chains, had been a mental torture far harder to endure than the actual physical pain.

I stand in the velvet darkness for a moment, collecting myself. The air here is gentle, layered with the fragrant scents of the Generalife, the Alhambra gardens. I wait for the peace to settle my soul.

But it doesn't.

Someone is here.

I feel it on the air like I did the memories of pain only moments earlier. I sense it, a faint ripple in the atmosphere, a presence somewhere nearby. I turn slowly, my eyes scanning every stone and leaf for a shadow, a hint of whoever is close by. I can smell them, an odd spice that is vaguely familiar, but elusive. I close my eyes and allow myself to feel my way into it, for the impressions to reach me rather than my logical deductions take over.

Blood. Running. Grief.

They come as sensations rather than words. A battlefield. A hundred battlefields. Dark nights and empty bottles. I know this presence like a brother.

My eyes fly open, and I spin around. "Guidry," I say roughly. "Show yourself, you bastard."

CHAPTER 7

GUIDRY

Mississippi, 1731
Guidry

On a dark bayou night when Guidry de Ainhoa was twenty-two, he lost everyone he loved, and gained immortality.

After a Natchez attack on one of their garrisons, the French army took savage revenge on Guidry's village. As was the right of all women born into the matriarchal Natchez clan, Guidry's wife insisted on fighting at his side. Whilst Guidry swung his axe until blood drenched the earth, his wife wielded her blade with equal determination. As the Mississippi bayou burned and all around them fell, they thrust their children behind them, fighting and screaming their defiance until their hut was the last standing. The last thing Guidry would later recall was a French soldier hurling himself at his neck, and a searing agony across his throat that felt like death had come for him. Before the darkness fell, he saw his wife's head torn from her shoulders, and the last spark of life fading from his children's terrified eyes.

He woke to find his dead wife and children lying barely feet from his own body. Guidry knew that he had failed them. He understood that he was, at his very core, a failure as a man. He should have sent his wife and children to safety, should never have bowed to his wife's wishes to fight. It was his fault they were all dead.

Wishing only to join them, he closed his eyes and willed himself into the abyss.

Then he heard a woman's voice. "Guidry," she whispered. "Guidry, wake up."

Guidry tried to shut the voice out. He had no desire to wake ever again. He had failed to protect those he loved. He could not face the pain and emptiness of their absence, nor the crippling shame of his own inadequacy.

"Guidry!" The whisper was more insistent this time. "Hold on. Please. Wait. Wait for me." Her voice reached into the abyss, bringing with it a scent of vanilla, amber, and wildflowers so otherworldly that Guidry at first thought he must already be in the afterlife. Then he became aware of the pain of his physical body, and knew he lived still. He reached again for death, but that scent seemed to stand between him and the abyss. It infused his being with warmth and strength, whilst the woman's voice echoed inside him, a strange cord linking him to life itself. "Live, Guidry," she whispered. "Live. Wait for me."

The voice faded, but still, he could hear it's echo inside, feel her warming scent in the air around him.

Someone lifted him from where he lay. Too weak to resist, he was borne across the burning, ravaged landscape of his village as if he were flying. His body, wracked with agony, was laid down in a clearing deep in the forest, far from the cries of men. A strange liquid, like the most potent and intoxicating wine, slipped down his throat, healing him, changing him in some fundamental way. He wanted the lifegiving draught to stop, and he wanted it to never end. He could still see the peaceful abyss of death. But with every mouthful the abyss shrank, and the force inside him grew, pulling him reluctantly back to life.

Afterwards, he would try to recall how it had happened, but he never could. All he knew was that when finally he returned to consciousness, he was transformed. His rescuer had remade him.

The immortality part took some time to understand. At first Guidry knew only that he could now change form into that of a wolf. Even for a warrior born into the Natchez people of Mississippi, that was difficult enough to comprehend. He was also driven by a terrible, wracking thirst.

"You must drink blood before the sun rises, if you are to live," said the man who had carried Guidry from the village. Guidry did not question him; the lust for blood was a burning need that overcame even his own desire for death. They ran together through the night toward the French garrison. The man who had saved him ran at his side, though he was not in animal form.

Before dawn was fully broken, Guidry found the French soldier who had murdered his wife and children. The soldier was insensible with wine and the aftermath of violence, sitting alone by a fire, his face still covered in the blood of those Guidry had loved. Guidry lurked in the shadows and then came at him from behind. The soldier was dead before he ever knew what had taken his life. Guidry drained his body to no more than a limp rag, and then he fled into the forest. The woman's voice he had heard whilst deep in the abyss between life and death was gone now, but the memory of it pulled at the edges of his conscious mind, the strange scent lingering like a tantalising ghost on the air, just beyond reach.

Later that night he sat by a fire across from Antoine

Marigny, the man who had fed Guidry the blood that had brought him back from death. Guidry was wearing clothes Antoine had given him and eating meat the other had cooked, but both could have been ashes, so deep and complete was Guidry's agony. "Am I the same as you, now?" He asked, dully.

"No." Antoine shook his head slowly. "You are—something else, I think. You did not die before I gave you the blood, and you do not appear to need more of it. Nor can my kind change their form to wolf."

"I know who—and what— you are. Our people have spoken of you before. I know you are a vampire." Guidry said the words without emotion. He thought he might never feel anything, really, again.

"Yes." Antoine met his eyes steadily. "The attack on your village was my fault, if not my doing."

Guidry made a harsh noise. "Do not speak to me of fault." He saw his wife's blood-soaked face, her fear filled eyes as she stood so bravely before that final, terrible assault. "The failure is mine. And besides, it was not you who attacked the French garrison, and brought their fury upon our village."

Antoine made an impatient noise. "The man responsible for that attack is a vampire whom I created. The fault is mine."

"Is that why you saved me?" Guidry traced the livid scar across his throat as he asked the question. "To assuage your own guilt? No man should survive such a wound." He paused. "I wish I had not."

"Then I am sorry." Antoine frowned. "I know something of what it is to live when you wish only for death."

"But now I am not only alive. I am—this." Guidry gestured at his dirt covered body. "Will I always want blood?"

"Do you crave it now?"

"No." Guidry grimaced. "Even the thought of it sickens me."

"Then I don't believe you ever will again." Antoine shook his head. "I don't entirely know what my blood made you, or why you craved human blood on awakening. I intended only to save your life, not to change your form. I thought perhaps there might be answers to your current form in your own stories, in Natchez mythology."

Guidry shook his head. "Not for this."

"I have heard that your people can shape shift to animal form."

"In spirit, perhaps. In ceremony we might share the form of a willing animal for a time. But of this, of physically becoming a wolf, I know nothing." Guidry stared around at the silent forest. The smell of the charred remnants of the fire that had burned his village clung to his hair, turning his stomach. "I will not stay here. I cannot."

"Where will you go?"

"Across the sea. To the place where the Frenchmen came from. Perhaps there, I will find people who understand what I have become." He threw a stick into the fire. "And perhaps there, I will not see my wife and children die with every breath I take."

Antoine flinched but didn't speak.

"When you saved me," Guidry said slowly, frowning into the fire, "Did you see a woman? One of your people, I think. She was calling to me."

Antoine frowned. "There were none of your people left alive in the village. And there are no French women for at least a hundred miles."

"She was there." Guidry could still feel her scent warm in the air around him, like a tantalising ghost that was just out of reach. "I felt her, close by."

"I didn't see anyone." Antoine paused. "But I did feel—something. I can't explain it, exactly. But I knew I could save you." He shook his head. "I knew I *must* save you. I don't understand it," he said wearily. "But it seems, of late, that there is much I do not understand."

"Then come with me." Guidry met his eyes across the fire. "I know nothing of your world. Your people. I will be lost in that world without help. And it seems to me that neither of us have anything left to live for here."

Antoine's eyes narrowed. "You wish to travel with me," he said flatly. "Even knowing what I am?"

"You are a vampire." Guidry shrugged. "I change into a wolf, it seems. Neither of us are likely to find friends among normal men, are we?"

Antoine gave a low cough of laughter. "No. I suppose in that, you are correct."

"Your kind," Guidry said. "You live forever, do you not?"

The other man's face darkened. "So it would seem," he said shortly.

"Then that, at least, is something I have to my advantage." Guidry stood up. "I plan to die at the earliest opportunity. And next time death comes for me, you will not thwart it. Are we agreed?" He put out his arm, and Antoine took it.

In the morning the two were gone, to the coast, and to the Old World.

But death, despite his best efforts, did not come for Guidry de Ainhoa.

The first time he realized his own immortality was in the French Pyrenees. He had gone out hunting, in wolf form. Antoine was in Paris, where he owned a lavish house frequented by those who enjoyed all manner of debauchery. Guidry preferred the wilderness of mountains, of places where people were not. That part of his nature was unchanged from his human life. The Pyrenees were utterly different to the flat bayou country of his birth, but they were exhilarating, too. He lived a peaceful enough life. Until the day he encountered a wolf pack.

The wolves were not shapeshifters, as he was. These were hungry beasts who survived in a dangerous world that wanted only to kill them. They were suspicious of the strange interloper, and they had learned early to eliminate any threat that might prove to be an enemy.

They tore Guidry's body to pieces.

Guidry awoke, naked and in human form, in the same place the pack had taken him down, his broken body miraculously healed.

At first, he could not quite believe it. Perhaps, he thought, the wolves had not attacked him as badly as he thought. But he could make no sense of it. He began courting death, coming ever closer to men with their knives and hunting bows, daring them to kill him. Some months later, one did. Guidry saw the arrow come for him. Saw it enter his own heart.

That second time, when Guidry woke from death, he knew what he had before only suspected: he could not be killed. The hunter who had shot him in wolf form was now staring down at Guidry's naked human form in fascinated horror. Guidry killed him with the man's own knife. He knew instinctively that such secrets were dangerous for any man to know.

Time wore on, and he met others of his kind, who could shift from man to wolf. Some had been made deliberately, though that was a rare and dark magic. Most had been born into a pack. All of them lived longer than normal men, often well over a century.

But they all aged. All died. And Guidry never met one who had been created by taking the blood of a vampire.

Guidry did not age a single day. He was killed more times than he could remember. Every time, without fail, he was reborn.

He didn't speak to anyone about his immortality, even Antoine, who remained his closest friend. Antoine never questioned Guidry's unchanging appearance, and Guidry never offered explanations. The two rarely spoke of the life they had left behind. Antoine used his powers of compulsion over humans to grant them both new identities. Guidry became the

Count de Ainhoa, a Basque nobleman with vast estates in the Pyrenees. Antoine became a French Viscount, a *Vicomte*, in Provence. Together they traveled as far as India, amassing impenetrable fortunes that helped them create new identities. Hidden behind a well-constructed front of respectable business, they built another, darker venture: a well disguised mercenary business. Sometimes they were assassin, other times saviour. They rescued some, and dispatched others, mostly for coin but occasionally, simply to right what they thought of as a wrong. They became adept in the acquiring of intelligence, cultivating contacts high in governments around the world. Often, they dealt in blood and death, for it was what they both knew, and what they excelled at.

Over time, Guidry's memory of his family's horrific death faded, though never his knowledge of his own inadequacy. The woman he had once loved became a fond memory, his children cherished whispers on the wind. He let them go, for he knew they were at peace in the world of spirit, whilst he still raged in the world of men. His guilt and shame hardened into an iron strength, like the nacre of a pearl growing around an irritant. Whilst he could not change the past, Guidry found himself very willing to exercise his skill at bringing death in any cause he felt just. Sometimes it was to assist the victims of brutality, whether protecting a starving street urchin, or saving women and children from the guillotine during the French Revolution. Sometimes he killed men who had committed acts he considered evil. He thought nothing of bringing such death and did not plague himself with thoughts of moral right, just as he did not hesitate to pay for women when the need took him. Love and death were the irritants around which the pearl of his soul had grown. But the years had granted many layers of nacre between he and that original wound. Guidry treated both with cold detachment. Love, he knew, was not meant for him.

He thought often of the strange whispers he had heard the

night Antoine had saved him, and many times, he thought he caught the faintest hint of the amber and vanilla scent that had filled his soul that night. But never did he see anyone to whom either might belong. At times when he woke from tortured dreams wracked with harsh, almost painful desire, and a longing he couldn't name, both the scent and the voice seemed to hang in the air about him, as if they had been real only moments before he woke.

Over the years, he decided that the scent and the woman's voice must belong to some form of God, a strange call from whatever otherworld it was that governed supernatural creatures such as himself. Something must have wanted him to become what he was, though he had long since given up hoping to be shown a purpose. If his years on earth had taught Guidry anything, it was that no human had a purpose. People were born; they lived; they died. Some lived good lives, but these, in Guidry's experience, were few and far between. Since the day he was turned in 1731 until the day in which he now found himself, in 1810, Guidry had seen plague, famine, and more wars than he knew how to count. He had seen children die of starvation and men murder each other for no reason other than the coin they were being paid. He no longer expected the world to be a good place. He certainly didn't wish for love. He would never again suffer the agony of watching the woman he loved die; and after all these years, he knew that for him, love could end in no other way. What comfort he found in women was bought with coin and gone with the dawn.

He followed war as other men did gold, always with an impersonal detachment. War was business for Guidry. But in 1808, Napoleon's armies crossed Guidry's lands on their way through the Pyrenees to invade Spain. War had once again become personal.

As he had almost a century ago, Guidry watched French soldiers take all in their path, raping land and women with callous disregard for the lives they destroyed. Perhaps it was a lingering hatred of the men who had once ransacked his village. Perhaps it was a growing disgust with the bloodshed France had suffered during the revolution, and in the aftermath. Either way, Guidry found himself fighting against the French. Rather than joining the regular Spanish army to fight what would become known as Spain's War for Independence, he found his unique skills better suited to the small bands of Spanish rebels, or *guerilleros*. Later, when the British joined the fight against the French, the guerilleros became better organized and more effective. Guidry and Antoine, as they always had, gathered intelligence and, with others who possessed similar supernatural abilities, created their own informal network to aid the rebels in their cause.

Thus it was that in April 1810, Guidry found himself bedding down amongst some trees thirty miles north of the Andalucian city of Granada, the night before a battle against the French. He fell into sleep with the ease of a man who had known many rougher beds.

This night, however, Guidry's sleep was not destined to be peaceful.

It was the scent that hit him first. That tantalising haze of musk and vanilla, shot through with wildflowers.

He could feel a presence in the dream, like a shadow just out of his peripheral vision. He wanted to clutch onto that presence, force her to become material, capture the maddening spectre that had haunted his nights for as long as his immortal life. But she was ephemeral, and no matter how he ran toward her, it seemed shimmering lights divided them.

He woke in a rush of savage lust that took the breath from his body and made even the hard ground seem too hot for comfort.

Guidry rolled over, masking his arousal from the guerilleros sprawled around him as he splashed water over his face, his heart still thudding uncontrollably.

The sentry slipped through the trees to his side. "The French are coming," he murmured in Guidry's ear.

"Good," Guidry snarled, with enough vehemence to make the sentry step back, rather startled. "I'll bring my people around the trees," Guidry went on, not bothering to modify his tone. "We'll harass their rear lines."

The man didn't ask who Guidry's 'people' were, and Guidry didn't offer an explanation. The truth was that he alone was 'the people'. And right now, he needed the savagery of his wolfish form, and the release of ripping French flesh from limb to limb.

Anything, he thought as he moved deep into the trees and shifted form, *to wipe the craving for that scent from my mind, and this uncontrollable need from my body.*

But instead of dulling his body, his wolf form only heightened Guidry's senses. As he loped across the night dark ground toward the approaching French lines, the haunting scent seemed to hang on the air around him, clouding his mind and firing every nerve in his body.

Launching himself at the first blue uniform he saw, Guidry found himself fighting almost mechanically, if with ruthless efficiency.

Another part of his mind, however, was lost in the sensuality of his dream, and the unerring sense that the woman was somehow close by.

Who are you? Guidry asked as his teeth sank into yet another neck, felling the Frenchman with savage ease.

But the night held only blood, not answers. Perhaps, he thought grimly as he wreaked havoc on the French rearguard, the strange presence that haunted his dreams was some long suppressed part of his conscience torturing him. Or, if he held to the beliefs of his ancestors, a vengeful deity holding him accountable for a life that had been anything other than free of sin.

He shut out any thought of the emotions the scent aroused in him. He had no desire in feeling anything that might pierce the layers time had grown around his heart.

Love, Guidry de Ainhoa well knew, would never find him again. He would not allow it.

He fought grimly through the night, using the familiar comfort of steel and blood to escape the troubling emotions aroused by that maddening scent.

CHAPTER 8

DAWN

Harper

$\mathcal{I}$ wake in the early hours to find Antoine gone.

We hunted earlier, drank together in a village some miles from here. We made love under an open sky, and then returned to the house and gazed upon our sleeping daughters before going to bed. We had avoided speaking of the conversations that must be had. I have sensed Antoine's discomfort in being here, but I know my husband well enough to know he will speak when he is ready, and not a moment before.

Now he is gone, and the unease that has stalked me since our arrival has grown into a gnawing fear.

I make a cup of tea and take it up to the terrace. Dawn is still a few hours away. The Alhambra slumbers on the hill opposite, ancient, mysterious, and somehow dangerous.

I know that is where Antoine has gone. Whatever horrors he endured in that place are a darkness he carries inside him that even I cannot penetrate. Guidry, perhaps, was the only person who truly understood what he endured there, but Guidry is gone, vanished from our lives as if he never was. The last time I saw him was the night I destroyed Keziah, the ancient vampire who originally turned Antoine. Our twins were newborns then, and, we feared, lost forever in the waterpaths with Callie. Then Jeremiah had gone into the waterpaths, to find Callie, and send our girls home to us. We know he did the latter, but neither he nor Callie ever returned.

It was Guidry who had known our twins were in Revolutionary Paris. He had known a great many things, I believe, about Callie, Jeremiah, and our twins, but he shared none of that information with us, despite owing Antoine his life and having been at his side for more than two centuries. After we got the twins back, I had forgiven him his silence, or at least I thought I had. But as the years have passed, and my own corrosive fears for the safety of our daughters have grown, that forgiveness has eroded away, replaced by a hard, cold anger. Guidry is the only person who might have answers to the questions that plague Antoine and me. For more than two hundred years, he ran at Antoine's side like a brother, his closest companion, more trusted even than Tate, Antoine's oldest companion. And yet at the moment we needed him the most, he abandoned us all. Even if I could find it in myself to understand his decision, I can never forgive him for abandoning Antoine. The hole his absence has left in Antoine's heart is one that can't be filled, not by Tate, me, or even the twins. Guidry was the person Antoine trusted the most in this world. Now, I know, he wonders if that relationship was ever real at all. Was Guidry truly Antoine's friend, or did he have another agenda, all along? Did he have reasons of his own for wanting to see our daughters born safe? Was he working toward another goal, all that time, one we don't understand? And if so, what is it, and what does it have to do with our daughters?

I swallow a hot mouthful of tea and almost relish the scalding pain as it burns down my throat. These questions are both pointless and horribly repetitive. I rarely allow myself to indulge them. The only certainty is that they are questions only Guidry can answer—and he clearly has no intention of doing so. Not so much as a trace of him has been found in all these years, and I know how hard Antoine has looked. He disappeared as effectively as did any evidence of Jeremiah and Callie's life. Other than Antoine's deduction that he once met their daughter, a girl called Calliope Perrault, in Regency London, we know nothing of Callie and Jeremiah's fate.

I can't help but feel the silence is intentional. Jeremiah would have left word for Antoine if he could have. He knew how much we all loved him and Callie. He would never have left us wondering like this, unless there was good reason.

And I cannot help but suspect that the reason for this suffocating, oppressive blanket of silence from the past, is because our daughters somehow still have a part to play in it. And that thought terrifies me more than any other.

There is a soft thud nearby. "Antoine," I say softly.

He emerges from the gloom, his face cut through with grim lines, his ancient soul for once writ large in his dark eyes. He reaches into a terracotta pot for the inevitable bottle of whiskey and swallows it in deep gulps that make me nervous. He takes the seat next to me, the uncapped bottle still in his hand. "Guidry is here," he says without preamble.

I am unable to move, the teacup listing sideways in my hand, its contents forgotten. "Here," I whisper. "He's here, now?" I swallow, trying to breathe, my body alternately hot and freezing cold. "Did you speak to him?"

"No." Antoine shakes his head abruptly and takes another swallow of whiskey. "I went to the Alhambra, to the dungeons." He casts his eyes sideways. I nod, not needing him to explain, and he continues. "I sensed him. Close by. Close enough to touch, I'd think. But by the time I realized who it was I sensed, he was gone. I couldn't even track him, though I tried." He shakes his head again, this time in disgust. "Guidry always was a master of disguise. If he doesn't want to be found, I won't find him. As we already know."

I can hear the frustration in his voice, but I sense something else, too, the loneliness he has tried so hard to deny all these years. Whether Antoine wants to admit it or not, he misses Guidry, perhaps as much as I still miss my dead twin sister, Tessa. Maybe more, given the centuries they spent at one another's side.

"Why would he come, now, after all this time?" I stare out over the valley at the ochre towers of the Alhambra, my eyes lingering on the raw scar in the mountain below, a remnant of the French occupation. Napoleon's forces set explosives all through the palaces when they retreated. The ensuing blast would have destroyed the Alhambra entirely, had it not been for the heroic actions of a Spanish soldier, who cut the wires. The huge hole in the slope below the Alhambra is a living memory of the destruction. Somehow the unhealed scar feels representative of our family's relationship with this place, and that era. My question to Antoine is almost rhetorical.

I know why Guidry is here, now, in this time.

The paths of past and present entwine here. Whatever mysteries have dogged us all these years, the answers lie here, in Granada. I can't help but feel that the time of reckoning is approaching. The thought terrifies me.

"Something is coming." Antoine's grim tone mirrors my own thoughts. "Whatever it is that Guidry ran from telling us all those years ago must be about to unfold."

"Can't we stop it?" I know the futility of my question even as I ask it. *How does anyone stop the future from unfolding?*

Antoine makes a frustrated noise. "Not unless we lock our daughters into a padded cell and throw away the key." His face cracks into a wry semblance of a smile. "And don't think I haven't thought of it, more than once."

I give a silent huff of laughter and cover his hand with my

own. He grips my fingers tightly, and we sit in silence, watching the sky gradually pale with the first silver threads of dawn.

"Do you still want to go to the Alhambra today?" I ask eventually, as gold gleams on the horizon. "I could make excuses to Marguerite if you like. I know Aurelia isn't keen on the idea."

"I noticed." Antoine frowns. "Why is that, do you think?"

"I don't know." I shake my head. "You know as well as I do that the twins keep their secrets from us. And if Aurelia was going to tell anyone, it would be you, not me."

"Hardly." Antoine tosses off his glass. "You overestimate our relationship, Harper. You always have. Aurelia may enjoy testing her sword arm against mine, but we don't share secrets. She's as much a mystery to me as she is to you. So is Marguerite, for that matter." He leans forward, elbows on his knees. "How is it that we have two daughters," he says quietly, "who I feel like I don't know at all? Do you think this happens to all parents, or is it just us?"

"There's hardly a book I can read that deals with vampire parents raising time traveling twins." I mean it as a joke, but there is a wealth of sadness behind the remark that even I can't disguise. Antoine grips my hand, and for a time, we don't speak. Then, as the predawn gives way to sunrise, he turns to me.

"Do we tell them about Guidry being here?" He searches my face, the uncertainty in his own making my heart ache. "Or do we keep it to ourselves?"

I take a deep breath. "We tell them," I say, my voice nonetheless shaking slightly. "Tonight, when Tate and the others arrive, we tell them the whole damned thing. And we pray that they forgive us for keeping secrets this long."

Antoine nods slowly. "Tonight, then," he says, and I hear the note of decision in his voice. He sits back in his chair, and we watch the day grow together.

It is the 20th of March. Tonight will mark twenty-one years that the girls have been alive— in our time, at least.

CHAPTER 9

MONASTERY

Harper

$\mathcal{M}$arguerite's tour isn't until late afternoon, so in the morning we all go for churros and chocolate, then walk home along the Calle del Tristes, by the river Darro.

"Why is it called the street of sadness?" I ask Antoine as we walk.

"Traditionally, it was the route taken by funeral processions, from the Cathedral to the cemetery." His mouth tightens momentarily. "A lot of tears have been shed here, over the years." His eyes flicker sideways, across the river, where wilderness has grown over ancient, crumbling stone. "In Granada," he says quietly, his eyes lingering on the stone, "secrets and mystery live in every corner. This city has seen more violence, beauty, and brilliance than perhaps any other in Europe."

"Careful, Dad." Marguerite's eyes sparkle as she links her arm through her father's. "For a moment there it almost sounded as if you like the place."

Antoine gives a gruff cough of laughter, but his eyes soften as he tucks his daughter's arm through his. "It does have its charms, I'll confess." He nods at a small arch window cut into the wall of an old monastery to our left. The window is covered by a wooden shutter. A sign on the wall advertises sweets for five euros. "For example," Antoine says, "knock on that shutter." He stifles a grin as he gives Marguerite a ten euro note. "Give that to the nun who opens it."

"Oh, come on." Aurelia looks mildly amused. "Marguerite is an historian. Surely, she knows about the nuns."

"Actually," Marguerite says, looking between them, "I don't." She shrugs rather self-consciously. "I tend to be rather one eyed in what I study."

"Ha." Aurelia's eyes gleam. "Then come with me." I take Marguerite's place beside Antoine and follow the two girls at a slight distance as they approach the wooden shutter and rap on it.

The shutter opens, and a wrinkled, ancient hand reaches out and plucks the ten euro note from Marguerite's hand. A moment later a cellophane bag is pushed across the small wooden opening. It contains a mixture of sweets and biscuits, clearly handmade. Not a word is exchanged, and the shutter slams closed as soon as the girls take the bag.

"What Dad didn't tell you," Aurelia says, grinning mischievously, "is that it doesn't matter if you hand the nuns one hundred euros or five, the bag of sweets is the same—and no change is ever given. What's more, it's a silent order of nuns, so there's absolutely no point in arguing with them."

Marguerite looks as enchanted as I feel. "I love this place so much," she says wistfully. "It's like every stone has a story here."

We are turning to walk away when the shutter behind us opens once again, and an old, cracked voice says a word that stops me in my tracks, and sends chills down my spine: *"Sangre."*

Blood.

It's one of the first words I learned in another language,

years ago when Keziah took me to South America. To hear it now, here, on the lips of a nun sworn to silence, feels ominous, to say the least. Antoine tenses beside me, coiled and ready for defense. "Get away from there," he orders the girls curtly, his eyes scanning the cobblestoned street for potential threats. But the street is largely empty, and the girls, ignoring their father, are already moving toward the window. Antoine shakes his head in annoyance and strides toward them, me at his side.

A wimpled nun peers out at us from the small arched window. Her face is wizened and lined, her blue eyes faded and rheumy, skin translucent as rice paper. A gnarled hand reaches through the window, and as Marguerite and Aurelia get closer, I realize the nun is staring at the pendants around their necks.

Pendants that are usually tucked beneath a blouse or resting quietly on their chests.

Now, however, the pendants are hovering in midair, lifting from the girls' bodies as if reaching toward the woman's hand. The contents of the pendants are a mystery to us beyond our belief they contain a combination of my human blood, taken before the girls were born, and Antoine's vampiric blood. Now the ruby liquid swirls inside the glass and filigree pendants like a living thing. Strange silver and gold lights flash in their depths, like a universe trying to escape.

The nun's hand reaches like a claw toward the pendants, and she presses her forehead against the stone arch, as if trying to push herself through it. She is muttering something over and over. As I come closer, her words become clearer: *"Porque la vida de la carne en la sangre está,"* she mutters, her eyes gleaming with a strange light as she strains through the arch. *For the life of the flesh is in the blood.*

"It's Leviticus 17:11," Antoine mutters, more to himself than me. "Girls," he says, this time more forcefully. "Get back from there."

But Aurelia and Marguerite ignore him as if he isn't there,

and I get the terrible sense that even if they wished to obey, they are caught up in a force beyond themselves. *"Que vida?"* Marguerite whispers, leaning toward the window. *What life?*

"Immortalidad?" Aurelia asks at the same time, and I feel my heart seize with a terrible, painful sympathy. My daughter is asking if the blood means immortality. For all that Antoine and I have been pondering that question, it is heartbreaking to realize that the girls, too, must live daily with the uncertainty of their own mortality.

The nun's eyes gleam with a sudden, sharp light. *"Un sorbo de sangre,"* she mutters, her eyes fixed on the pendant. *"Debes tomar un sorbo de sangre."*

My heart seizes with fear. I understand the nun's words all too well.

A sip of blood. You must take a sip of blood.

CHAPTER 10

POOL

Aurelia

There is a hard, predatory gleam in the nun's eyes as she leans toward Marguerite and I. To me there is something chilling, almost inhuman, about her presence. *"Toma lo que quieras,"* she rasps, *"y pagarás por ello." Take what you want, and pay for it.*

I hear Mom gasp behind us and feel, rather than see, Dad reach for us.

But they are both too late.

My pendant flashes a sudden, savage gold. The scent of pine and fir fills my senses, and I'm hit by a bolt of longing like the bittersweet poignancy of homesickness. I grip Marguerite's hand so hard she winces. Then the pendant stabs my skin with a blazing heat that is almost painful, and for a terrible moment I think the vial at my neck will explode.

The sharp physical sensation is enough to jolt me out of the strange trance and bring the danger of our situation into hard focus. Marguerite's hand in mine feels soft, insubstantial. She is fading, the waterpaths drawing her onward. Fear drives my curiosity into the shadows. Sucking in a deep breath I grip my twin tightly, drawing her back, away from the waterpaths' treacherous pull. But she has moved even closer to the window, her pendant now so close to the nun's bony finger that bare millimeters separate the two. I know, with a horrible, sickening certainty, that true danger lies in that connection. I don't know how I know it. I just do.

Get her away from that nun.

I close my eyes, and allow the water paths to take us both.

Except they don't.

At first I think we are falling into the past. There is the disorientation of slipping into dark chaos, the shimmering lights all around. But we do not tumble entirely into the familiar, deceptive morass. One moment we are falling; the next we are standing in a medieval courtyard, at the end of a long, shallow pool of water. It is nighttime, and the scent of pine and fir fills my senses, undercut by another, more acrid, smell.

I look around, frowning. "I know this place."

"Of course you do." Marguerite sounds slightly impatient. "It's the Casa de Zafra, behind the monastery. It used to accommodate the nuns. In our time they use it as a tourist center during the day." She looks around warily. "I'm not sure about now."

I catch a metallic gleam in the corner and squeeze her hand. "I don't think we've traveled in time." I raise our joined hands and point at the sign, which has a digital code tourists can scan to get an audio tour.

"If we haven't traveled in time," Marguerite whispers, "then why are we here?"

"I don't know." I inhale again, the scent so strong this time it makes me weak at the knees. "Can you smell that?"

Marguerite looks at me strangely. "You mean you can smell that, too? Like a strange forest."

"Pine and fir," I say. "With gunpowder."

"Like yew and berries, with some kind of sulfur," says Marguerite at the same time. We stare at each other.

"Different scents." I frown, trying to puzzle it out.

Marguerite tilts her head. "Different pathways?"

As she speaks, the water in front of us begins to bubble, then to roil. Marguerite's hand is still in mine. I want to draw her away from the water, but I'm as helpless to move as she seems to be. Strange golden flashes light the water from beneath. It's like looking down into the waterpaths instead of being immersed in them. For someone who has traveled amid that chaos many times, it is a strange, disembodied experience, like gazing into the proverbial looking glass. The whispers rise from the water, swirling around me, as incoherent as ever but more compelling than I've ever felt them. The water itself seems to swirl with the sound, forming and reforming the odd golden threads into shapes that look almost human. I can't look away from the pool, or from the gold that seems to writhe through it like a living thing. As I watch, the water and gold combine into a trick of shadow and light to form a man's face.

It is indistinct, the features not entirely clear, but I know it from my dreams the same way I know the scent, viscerally, in some animal part of my soul. It's a presence, a feeling, rather than any particular structure or shape. I could not redraw the face, but I know it like I do my own being. It reaches for me with the desperate, aching longing I feel in my dreams, and every cell of my body answers the call, any thought of resistance useless.

It's only when I feel Marguerite falling that I snap back into focus. It takes a monumental effort of will to open my eyes.

Marguerite is teetering on the edge of the pool, her face rippling and indistinct.

"Marguerite!" My sharp cry cuts through her trance. To my relief her body solidifies once more. When she turns to me, her eyes are wide and terrified.

"Aurelia," she says, as I pull her back from the edge. "We must get out of here. These pathways don't lead to other times."

"What do you mean, they don't lead to other times?" My eyes swivel back to the water, to the golden fragments swirling in the depths. I have never wanted anything more than to follow their siren call, and plunge into the water.

Her voice is shrill. "Can't you see the silver in there?"

I look up, confused. "Silver?" I shake my head. "What do you mean?"

"The waterpaths in that pool don't lead to other times, Aurelia." She stares back at the water. "Those pathways lead to other worlds."

CHAPTER 11

LEVITICUS

Harper

The nun raises a bony finger and points at Aurelia and Marguerite, her face sharpening with malice. *"Toma lo que quieras, y pagarás por ello."* Take what you want, and pay for it.

A thrill of fear runs down my spine. The old Spanish proverb has never struck me as threatening, but the nun delivers it with the chilling resonance of a curse.

My girls lean toward her. The late afternoon sun bounces off the worn white tiles underfoot, so blinding that for a terrifying moment it seems to me that my daughters have disappeared. I blink, and there they are, still leaning in. My heart begins to beat again.

There is a flash of blue robes and a sound like the clatter of a chair falling. As suddenly as the nun appeared, she is gone. Before any of us have time to react, the wooden shutter is slammed shut in our faces by a younger, stronger hand. Clearly the nun's transgression has been spotted, and her withdrawal forced.

Just as abruptly, the two pendants float down to lay quietly

66

around the girls' necks, the brilliant swirl inside them fading toward their customary unremarkable dull red. Today, however, it seems to me as if a hint of the recent turbulence remains in the depths, like a slow-moving storm on a distant horizon. The girls themselves seem temporarily frozen. They are both pale, staring at the wooden shutter as if they heard something in the nun's words that I didn't.

I shiver. *It's my imagination.*

"We need to get out of here." Antoine is white faced and grim, scrutinizing every passerby with hard, wary eyes. The girls, who are still oddly quiet, give each other a look of mutual understanding that both touches me and makes me horribly aware of just how much they share that nobody else can ever be a part of.

We walk back up to the house in silence, none of us wanting to speak of dangerous topics in the open air. No sooner is the door to the carmen closed behind us, however, when the girls burst into excited chatter.

"That nun knew something." Marguerite's eyes shine. "And the pendants recognized her. She's connected to them, some-how. What do you think she meant by telling us to take a sip of blood? Or quoting that old proverb?"

"I'm more interested in that biblical passage," Aurelia cuts in, turning to Antoine. "Where did you say it was from, Dad? Leviticus?"

Antoine nods stiffly. I can tell he dislikes the entire discussion, but equally that he is as aware as I that we are inching ever closer to our moment of truth. In addition, this is the most our daughters have opened their private world to us in many years. I again have the terrible sense of destiny reaching for us, time closing like the snake of the ouroboros reaching, open jawed, for its own tail. "I will go back to the monastery after dark," Antoine says quietly. He glances at me, and I know what he means: before we tell the girls what we know about their past. "I'll find the nun, along with whatever she knows."

The girls both nod, but they aren't really listening. *"For the life of the flesh is in the blood."* Marguerite turns the words over slowly. Aurelia has already gone to the bookshelf and retrieved the bible there, but Antoine puts out his hand, stopping her as she would open it.

"You don't need to read it." His eyes are dark, face grim as he arrests Aurelia's hand on the pages. "I know the lines by heart. Any vampire who has ever questioned their origins has studied the entire chapter over and again. Particularly those final verses." He pauses, then begins:

"For the life of the flesh is in the blood: and I have given it to you upon the altar to make an atonement for your souls: for it is the blood that maketh an atonement for the soul.

Therefore, I said unto the children of Israel, no soul of you shall eat blood, neither shall any stranger that sojourneth among you eat blood."

For a moment we are all silent, absorbing the verse.

"Of course, its most common interpretation is in the dietary customs of Jews and Muslims," Antoine says finally. "The basis for the halal and kosher practice of draining animal flesh of blood before eating. But there has always been speculation, amongst our kind, that the verse applies to us specifically. That it refers to the practice of drinking blood, and thus prohibits vampires from taking the very thing we need to survive." He smiles without humor. "An earlier part of the chapter offers what some take as further evidence: *"And they shall no more offer their sacrifices unto devils, after whom they have gone a whoring."*

Aurelia is frowning. "You think that the devils referred to are vampires?"

Antoine shrugs. "I don't understand the bible any more than those who give their lifetimes over to scholarship of it. I'm not a theologian, and I gave up contemplating the reasons for our existence a long time ago; that way lies madness. But yes, I do believe it is possible that the passage refers to our kind. Why not?"

"Then why," says Marguerite, staring at the bible, "would a nun quote that line—then tell us we must take a sip of blood? Particularly in conjunction with that old proverb about taking what you want and paying for it."

I shudder. "I've never particularly liked that proverb. And that nun made it sound more like a curse than a promise."

Antoine's eyes on mine are full of the past we share, and the story we have lived together. "Curses and promises are remarkably similar, sometimes," he says softly, slipping his hand into mine. His strength is reassuring.

"What do you think it means?" I ask, studying his face.

Antoine shakes his head slowly. "I don't know," he says. "But I intend to find out."

CHAPTER 12

ALHAMBRA

Antoine

I'm impatient to revisit the monastery, but I know better than to infiltrate it in daylight. Vampires are creatures of the shadows, and our best work is done by night. We are also due for our Alhambra visit that afternoon, with Marguerite's student group. Beyond all those considerations, I'm more unsettled by the encounter with the nun than I'm willing to admit.

Not only because of her words, although those were chilling enough. I'm disturbed because the monastery of Santa Catalina de Zafra holds particular memories for me.

It was the first place I was taken, after my escape from the Alhambra. The Zafran sisters, as we called the nuns back then, were deeply enmeshed in the Spanish Independence movement against the French occupation. I remember little of my time there—but I do know that without the Zafran sisters, I would likely be dead. It was a nun who offered me her neck and bade me drink. But for her, I may not have survived my wounds, just as had it not been for

70

Guidry, I would never have made it out of the Alhambra at all.

It isn't possible that the nun in that window is the same one who fed me, back then. She would be long dead now. But religious orders are notorious for their memories, and their records. I imagine there is a memory of what took place back then, even if it is just an oral history. But even if that is true, it doesn't explain the nun's words, nor her connection to the pendants themselves. The way in which both pendants had floated toward her, and the strange malice in her eyes still makes my blood run cold hours later, as I follow my youngest daughter through the grounds of the Alhambra.

The palaces feel different in the daytime, alive with the sound of tourist chatter and the sonorous tones of guides. But although I listen to Marguerite's lecture like the attentive father I hope I am, I scan the crowds and every shadow for any sign of Guidry. I don't find any, of course, though I'm certain he's here. And the encounter with the nun has me even more convinced that his presence in Granada is no coincidence.

Although a large part of me wants to kill the bastard for the way he left us, another, traitorous part of me longs more than anything to see him again. Despite the secrets he quite clearly kept all the years we ran and fought together, even now I find myself reaching for the phone, or turning to share a joke with him, only to experience anew the terrible sense of loss his absence has left. Then I remind myself that whatever secrets he kept have something to do with my daughters, and I'm seized by such a killing rage that all I can see is blood.

I've felt the same internal conflict for twenty-one years. I doubt it will change any time soon. We're a fixed type of creature, vampires. Slow to passion, and even slower to forgiveness. The simple fact is that Guidry knew that Callie and Jeremiah would go back into the past. He even told Callie exactly where to go, and to whom. During the War of Independence in Spain,

Guidry was right here, working side by side with Jeremiah, who was known to me back then not by his name but only as the spy master and legendary code breaker, El Viajero. But I was a secondary player who worked more with the British army of the day than the Spanish rebels. It was Guidry who was here, who knew what happened back then, and exactly what role Jeremiah and Callie played.

I have spent twenty-one years wondering what else he knew—and why, despite ostensibly being my closest friend, he kept that knowledge from me for more than two centuries.

It had come as a tremendous shock for me to realize that the teenage Jeremiah Marigny I had met in 20th century Mississippi, would one day grow up to be the same El Viajero I had met two centuries before in Granada. A legendary spymaster and code-breaker, he had a distinct advantage when it came to the gathering of intelligence: a small army of supernatural creatures like Guidry who served the Spanish cause for Independence. The British army didn't know they were supernatural, of course. El Viajero was simply an anonymous Spaniard from whom came intelligence reports, filtered through the British agents, known as Guides, who went behind enemy lines.

El Viajero never made it into history books, and nor was he acknowledged for his extraordinary work in breaking Napoleon's codes. The credit for that went to George Scovell, the man to whom El Viajero had fed his information. Knowing Jeremiah as I later did, that doesn't surprise me. He was never one for glory.

I met El Viajero once only, on the same night I was rescued from the Alhambra dungeons. I didn't know his real name was Jeremiah Marigny. I certainly had no idea he was my own direct descendent, come from the future. How could I? Back then, if someone had told me that time travel was real, I would have thought them lost in an absinthe dream. Let alone if they had tried to tell me I would one day marry, and father time traveling twins. How could any man, even an immortal, believe such fantasy?

But understanding why he didn't try to tell me the truth doesn't lessen my regret, and my confusion. I still wonder why Jeremiah told me nothing then that might have helped me now. The last time I saw Jeremiah, before he went into the water-paths to bring our daughters home, he hated Guidry with an abiding passion, furious that Guidry had disappeared without telling us whatever he knew of Callie's whereabouts. And yet when I met him as El Viajero, Jeremiah was working closely with Guidry, and trusted him implicitly.

Why had he given me no hint at all, back then, that might help us now?

I glance at Aurelia, who is wearing a long skirt similar to her sister's. She's also carrying a small leather pack. I feel an odd tingle of alarm.

She looks like she has plans to go somewhere.

I try to quell my fears. My daughter might simply be dressing for drinks.

Or she's planning to go into the past.

As if to stoke my fears, I see the crumbling towers up ahead. I have a sudden vision of my daughters being caught up in the madness of those times, and despite my earlier visit, I can't suppress a shudder.

The acrid scent of gunpowder. Arkady's voice, manic with rage: "blow it all to hell . . ."

And just like that, I feel an overwhelming urge to tell my daughters everything.

What if they need it? I feel a sudden, destabilizing rush of fear. *What if hesitating now leaves them without information that may save her life?*

We are going to tell them anyway, tonight, I think. *There's no point hiding the truth. Not anymore.* And certainly not after the encounter with the nun. I can feel danger close, like a breath on my skin.

I think again of the night I spent in the company of El Viajero. *If only he had told me something,* I think, *anything at all, to prepare me, perhaps I would now be better equipped to help my girls face whatever is coming.*

Aurelia is coming. I clench my fists and brace myself.

It's time.

CHAPTER 13

PERFUME

Aurelia

It's late afternoon when we join Marguerite's tour of the Alhambra. Dad is grim faced, Mom pale and worried. They don't know we traveled, of course, and there's no chance either of us are about to tell them. All they saw was a faint shimmering as our forms begin to fade, and they've seen that happen enough times not to panic, or at least not visibly. Perhaps for a split second, they feared we were gone. But Marguerite and I mastered, long ago, the art of returning from the waterpaths to the exact moment we left. We came back just as the nun slammed the wooden shutter in our faces, and Dad ordered us away. The encounter had been strange enough to dominate the conversation on our return to the house, and thankfully to deflect our parent's questioning away from anything that might lead to Marguerite or I having to lie about our odd moment in the Casa Zafra. But I haven't stopped thinking about it since, and I'm sure Marguerite hasn't either.

Other worlds?

I spent the afternoon avoiding my parents' scrutiny by taking a long bath, during which I mulled over my sister's odd words. I needed solitude to think of what they might mean, where those pathways might lead. But no amount of thinking made sense of it, just as no amount of perfumed bathing could remove the disturbing scent of pine and fir from my nose. I am so disquieted that I have come to the tour wearing a long skirt over my suede trousers and boots, and carrying my 'travel bag', a small leather pack in which I have put all the basic things I might need if I land somewhere strange. Marguerite, I note, has done the same. We can both feel what is coming, and we've both had too much experience of landing in strange places and times to risk being caught unawares. I reach into my pack and surreptitiously spray some of my own perfume on my skin. It's called Goddess, a Spanish scent by Burberry. It's the one secret indulgence I always take into the past that I probably shouldn't. The past, however, is redolent with a great many odours that are pretty challenging to the modern nose. Wearing scent of any kind is forbidden in my unit, so when I'm home, I indulge in it all the time.. Especially right now, when I can't seem to breathe without smelling that strange forest scent. I touch my travel bag, feeling the knife in it with a sense of reassurance. A weapon is always a good idea when the waterpaths are close. Especially if I have to follow Marguerite somewhere odd.

Like, into another world.

I gulp another mouthful of water. I've been thirsty ever since we fell into the Casa de Zafra this afternoon, and I make a mental note to refill my bottle, which is already empty. I touch a plaque on the wall just outside the Alhambra entrance. It commemorates an invalid soldier, Jose Garcia, who risked his own life to cut the explosives the French left behind when they retreated from Granada after two years of occupying the city. As ever, I feel a poignant thrill at the bravery that saved such magnificent palaces being lost to the casual destruction of war.

I catch Dad watching me, his eyes dark. I know he fears my

love of war. The motto of my unit in the Spanish army is *Por Espana, me atrevo. For Spain, I dare.* It dates back to the Napoleonic wars, and the bands of rebels who made guerilla warfare against the French occupiers. My fascination and admiration for them is why I chose the Special Forces, of course. Dad knows that. He's never liked it. And I'd be lying if I said I don't gain some satisfaction from his discomfort.

I follow Marguerite along scented mosaic paths, through which water flows freely in channels and from ancient fountains. Marguerite catches my eye, and I see the same tremulous excitement I feel reflected in hers. *The waterpaths are close.*

I instinctively touch my pendant, which pulses even more heavily than before. *That nun knew something about our pendants. She was connected to them, somehow. And why did we travel to the Casa Zafra?*

"Are you still thinking about that bible verse?" It's Mom, hanging back slightly to walk at my side as the crowd moves ahead through the scented gardens of the Generalife. "The one the nun quoted?"

I nod. "I know Dad said a lot of vampires think it's referring to them." I glance sideways at Mom. "Like some kind of ancient warning. But I wonder if it means something else."

"You think it might have something to do with immortality." It isn't a question. And for once, I don't feel as if Mom is grasping at false reassurance, or trying to mask her own anxiety. She's quiet, serious, but at least she's not trying to protect me from her own fears. For once I feel like we're actually on the same page.

"I hope it does." I meet her eyes. "She told us we have to take a sip of blood."

"She also told you to take what you want, and pay for it." Mom shivers. "What do you imagine the payment for immortality is?"

I ignore that. "We have to try to find out what that nun actually knows."

Mom half smiles. "Just try and stop your father from going to that monastery tonight, and getting the truth out of that poor nun." She touches my arm and moves closer to where Marguerite is speaking. I go to stand by Dad, who's wearing a rather glazed expression.

"Antoine." I use his name, as I learned to do in public years ago, when we all began to look the same age. Dad visibly flinches. He hates us using his name, something that I confess I take a rather sadistic pleasure in doing. "Are you listening to a single word Marguerite is saying?"

He gives me a rather dry look. "And you've absorbed every word, I assume?"

I grin. "Actually, I was trying to work out where the French lay the explosives when they retreated." Expecting Dad to react with his customary wry humor, I'm slightly taken aback when he visibly stiffens. His eyes narrow, then he nods at the crumbling remnants of an old tower. "The first charges were laid beneath the Torre del Agua and the Torre del Cabo de la Carrera."

I take in his rigid stance, the fists balled white at his sides. But it's more than that. My father's eyes are darting this way and that, like a hunted animal. I've seen that look before, on fellow soldiers who revisit, either mentally or physically, particularly traumatic battlegrounds.

"You were here," I say flatly.

He nods, meeting my eyes briefly. "I was here." He pauses, as if making his mind up about something, then his lips tighten in decision and he turns to me. "There's a tunnel." He speaks quietly as we follow the tour group toward a yawning pit, into which, Marguerite is explaining, prisoners were once lowered by rope. "There's a whole network of tunnels, far beneath the Alhambra. The entrance to one of them is hidden by a large boulder on the banks of the Darro, across from the same monastery we visited today. The French didn't know about it; nobody did. It was one of the many secrets built into the Alhambra by the Moors. The tunnel comes out in the Alhambra at the Abencerrajes Palaces, behind a wall panel. It's how I got out—how we all did."

"How you got out." I repeat the words slowly, my eyes following the direction of his to where Marguerite is standing by the pit, and a sudden, horrible realization dawns. "The dungeons." *No wonder he never speaks about his time here.* I can't begin to imagine the terror of being lowered into that black cave. "You were a prisoner?"

"I was." He nods curtly. "And I would have died here. The man who caught us knew exactly what I was, and how to ensure I was too weak to fight back."

Frankincense, I think. It is the one thing able to cripple vampires. Whether burned, soaked into rope, taken in water, or impregnated in steel, frankincense is vampire kryptonite. Granada is a city, Dad once told me, in which many vampires have made their home over the years. A place where magic lives still, in the walls of the Alhambra, and the many cave dwellings in the hills nearby. The gypsies burn frankincense on every corner; they know well what monsters lurk in the shadows here.

Marguerite has moved on, but I'm still staring at the dark, yawning hole at my feet. It's a grim silo, about eleven metres across the opening, then dropping eight metres down to a small, dark space. Even the thought of my powerful, seemingly indestructible father being held in such a place makes me feel physically sick.

"Nobody knew we were here," Dad goes on, "nor who held us, or why." His voice is rough with pain that makes me think he's never spoken of this before; I can't help but wonder why he's telling me now. "Your mother and I will tell you more," he says quietly. "Tonight, when Tate and the others arrive." Uncle Tate is Dad's oldest friend, more like a brother. He's arriving with his wife, Iara. Our Uncle Connor will arrive with his wife Cass later tonight. Uncle Connor is a werewolf. The others are all vampires.

But right now all I can think of is that after all these years, all the toxic secrecy, Dad is finally offering to tell us the truth. I scrutinize his face for any sign of a lie, but I can't find one.

"You have my word," he says, clearly reading my mind. "The time for truth is long overdue. I thought silence would keep you safe, but I should have known better." He looks away, rubbing a hand over his face in an uncharacteristically impatient gesture. I've never seen him so tense.

I inhale deeply, stepping back from the pit, and suddenly I am surrounded by that scent again. Pine and fir, something wild and dangerous that makes my heart thud and my body flame. There is a flicker in my peripheral vision, an odd shadow, but when I try to focus on it, there is nothing there. The air shimmers oddly. I realize, with a lurch of fear, that Marguerite has led the tour group into the Court of Lions.

It's the fountain, I think. *That's why I'm smelling that scent. Why the air is shimmering. The fountain is calling me.*

"Tell me now." I turn to my father. "Tell me before we go into that place."

Dad frowns. "Why?"

I glance away. After a lifetime of Marguerite and I keeping each other's secrets, it is anathema to me to betray her. But my fear of doing so is overridden by that haunting scent. I have an overwhelming urge to lay everything at my father's feet, and hope, childish though it might be, that he can somehow solve our problems. "Marguerite told Mom that the reason she chose the Court of Lions for her dissertation was because the waterpaths leading to the time of his construction were closed to her."

"Harper told me." Dad is watching me closely as we slowly

trail the group.

"That's not entirely true." The air about me feels dense with that scent, the very atmosphere unstable. I stop just outside the Court. "You know the waterpaths whisper to us? Or should I say that there are certain places, or objects, where the waterpaths call us more strongly. Whispers come from those places, like an echo of other times."

I'm finding it difficult to speak. The waterpaths feel almost insidious, so close to the fountain. The pendant at my chest throbs with a sudden, savage heat.

"Yes." Dad's tone is sharp with the fear he and Mom always try to disguise. "That is, you told us, when you were little, that the whispers are stronger in some places than others."

But nowhere have they ever been strong like they are here. I inhale deeply, trying to breathe past that intoxicating scent and the heavy air. "We can travel without hearing them, if we focus hard enough, and especially if there's water nearby. Running water is better than still." I've never told him any of this, and I can see the fascination in his eyes. "I find the whispers . . .easier to resist than Marguerite. In fact, I actively avoid following them."

An image rises unbidden to mind, of an epitaph on a gravestone rendered indistinct by the centuries, standing in the place where only moments before, my teenage self had held a civil war soldier as the lifeblood drained from his body. I swore that would be the last time I would fall in love in the past, and even now the memory haunts me. I shut down the painful ghost and force myself to continue.

"We told you that some waterpaths are closed to us. What we didn't tell you is that is isn't only the pathways to certain time in the past that are closed."

My father frowns, clearly confused. "What other pathways are there?"

I take a deep breath. *Marguerite is going to kill me for this.*

"Pathways to other worlds," I say.

CHAPTER 14

LUCIA

Guidry
January 1810, Granada province

Guidry has been uneasy all day, and not just because of yesterday's battle against the French.

In fact, he had almost welcomed the battle for the alcazaba, even if the Spaniards had lost it. Anything to distract him from the endless disturbing dreams. Today he woke yet again on hard ground with his body even harder, wreathed in that maddening scent of amber, musk, vanilla and wildflowers.

Having always felt a cold anger against their French enemy, lately, as the war approaches Granada, Guidry finds his fury increasingly entwined with the lust and longing aroused by the strange scent. These past days the woman's presence has invaded his dreams more powerfully than it has in decades.

"The French will be in Granada in a matter of days." Lowering her eyeglass, Lucia Monteleagre props herself against a rock in the fading light. She commands a band of guerilleros based in the mountains around Granada and is one of the few such leaders Guidry truly respects.

"Not even a shot fired." Forcing himself to focus, Guidry stares in disgust at the battlements of the alcazaba as the Spanish flag is lowered, replaced a moment later by the French standard. *The Spanish flag,* he thinks savagely, *has fallen as easily as the rest of Andalucia seems likely to: with a sudden flutter of indignation that rapidly crumples into surrender.*

Two years ago, Lucia had been a wealthy heiress, destined for court and a titled marriage.

Then the French came.

Now, Lucia and her band of rebels, with their intimate knowledge of Spain's rugged mountain passes, wreak havoc on the rear guard of the advancing French army. They attack food supplies, steal weapons and horses, and pick off any stragglers. The French have begun to fear their attacks more than any formal battle with the regular Spanish army, which is highly disorganized.

"I need to get back to the finca and make a plan." Lucia turns determined brown eyes to Guidry. She is tall for a Spaniard, with the dark coloring of her Moorish heritage. "Do you think you can infiltrate the French rearguard again?"

Guidry nods, without explaining how he might accomplish that feat.

"Good." Lucia nods decisively. "Steal what communications you can. The French are using a new code, and the British have yet to crack it. Major Trembath will be meeting us in several days. Any communication you can steal from the French we will give to him. He is in contact with El Viajero, the code breaker."

"Trembath?" Guidry quirks a knowing eyebrow. "The good Major seems to find a lot of pressing business in Andalucia, lately."

"The British are the most valuable allies we have," Lucia says primly. "They are sending us an arms shipment soon, landing on the coast to the east of here." Despite her rather cold dignity, Guidry gains the satisfaction of seeing her olive skin take on a faintly reddish hue at the mention of Trembath's name.

"In fact," she goes on, "it's likely to be your friend, Antoine Marigny, who captains the ship." She casts Guidry a knowing look of her own. "I imagine it wouldn't be wise to set up the rendezvous with him in a church," she murmurs. "All that frankincense, after all."

It's Guidry's turn to look away. Smirking, Lucia creeps back from the rock and nods at the men hidden in the trees awaiting her signal. They melt back into the mountain paths that lead to the finca they use as a base. It's a small compound high in the mountains Lucia's family had once used as a base to graze the horses from which their fortune was derived. The fortune is gone now, along with Lucia's ancestral home in Granada. But many of the horses remain, though not even the French are fool or desperate enough to venture into the rugged mountains in search of them.

It is a strange quirk of Lucia's upbringing, in an ancient Spanish family with roots stretching back before even the Romans came, that paganism has been bred into her soul. Guidry has never shown her his wolf's face, nor Antoine betrayed his own nature. Lucia has never asked how Guidry manages to sneak into French camps entirely unnoticed, nor how Antoine can run a hundred miles from his ship on the coast to Granada in a single night. But she always ensures no frankincense is burned at the finca when Antoine is expected, and she never questions why Guidry often arrives naked, and keeps spare clothes in her stables. Lucia Monteleagre's priority is fighting the French invaders. Guidry suspects that she doesn't much care what manner of monsters he and Antoine are, so long as they are fighting on her side of the war.

Guidry slips through the smoke, bodies, and exhausted men of the French camp before anyone notices the black wolf in their midst. He catches the scent of leather and paper soon enough. Slipping into a canvas tent, he locates the satchel containing the French dispatches. Taking it, he is safely through the camp and loping toward the treeline when the scent hits him again.

Amber and musk. Vanilla and wildflowers.

It assails him in a wave of longing that sucks the breath from his lungs. Every nerve in his wolfish form is alight, aching and desiring in equal measure, his reaction so strong that his pace falters, his jaws nearly dropping the satchel.

He runs into the tree line, suppressing an animal urge to howl with longing. It's harder in this form to resist the urges that grip him, to endure the sudden, horrible intermingling of loneliness and desire. He compels himself to shift back into human form and dresses rapidly, staring about him in a vain attempt to find the source.

But the scent remains on the air, so tantalizingly close it seems he could reach out and touch it. And despite knowing the danger of lingering so close to the French camp, and his loyalty to Lucia and her cause, Guidry doesn't immediately run back to the finca. Instead, he finds the place where the scent seems the strongest, and curls himself into the trees to wait.

Until lately, Guidry thought that scent only ever existed in his dreams. But since the dreams have been coming thick and fast, so heady they feel overwhelming, he wakes with the scent all around him, permeating every place he finds himself. It sets his body afire and makes his heart ache, lost in desire for something, or someone, he doesn't even know. His fanciful ideas about a vengeful deity have begun to seem less fantasy, and more torturous reality.

"Come to me." He speaks aloud, and in English, a language he rarely uses in this place and time. His voice rasps with long suppressed emotion, his body filled with an almost unbearable longing. "Come to me," he says again, and he is unsure who it is he calls to.

And now the scent is here, all around him. Some indefinable wolfish instinct tells Guidry that whatever has haunted his dreams for decades is somewhere close by.

As dusk falls and the Spanish moon begins to rise over the distant mountains, Guidry hunkers down and waits, unsure for what, the words throbbing in his heart like a mantra:

Come to me.

CHAPTER 15

Aurelia
Present day

"Other worlds." Dad's face has visibly paled, his eyes flashing with the preternatural lights that warn of heightened emotion. "Do you mean to say you girls have actually traveled to these . . .other worlds?"

"No." I shake my head. "Or at least, I don't think so." Seeing his eyes darken with annoyance, I hurry on, trying to ignore the fierce pull of the fountain within, the strange silvery whispers I can already hear all around me. "I can't feel the pathways leading to those worlds like Marguerite can. Or that is, I can sense them, but only like . . .shadows, in the distance. Different things whisper to us both, from the waterpaths. What calls Marguerite is different from what calls me." I meet his eyes. "But regardless of the differences, something in that fountain is trying to call to us both. Something dangerous. And strong."

I feel a sense of shame, and betrayal, in laying these burdens at my father's door when there is nothing he can do to help us, nor any way he can follow us inside. *But this isn't about us,* I remind myself, as the whispers rise, and the scent of pine and fir begins to permeate the air about me. I force myself to resist the pull.

"It's Mom," I say, seeing the carefully guarded tension in Dad's eyes give way to something savage, his fists clenching involuntarily at his sides. *You did this,* I chide myself. *You brought his worst fears to life.*

"Sometimes Mom hears the waterpaths," I go on. "Marguerite wants to know if she can hear these ones, too. But I don't think Mom should be here, Dad. I don't think it's safe for her."

Marguerite is delivering the last of her lecture, her voice carrying clearly to where we stand. "In 1884, when the fountain's main basin was raised, a cylindrical marble block was discovered. Its top was pierced by many holes. Based on the description in Ibn Zamrak's poem inscribed on the basin, archeologists theorized that the holes were connected to a series of pipes that allowed water to flow both in and out of the basin at the same time."

*Flowing in and out . . . .*Her words feel prophetic, as if she's describing the pathways themselves, the doors that are closed to us both. I glance through the archways at the fountain. Perhaps it is the growing twilight, or the uplights set into the marble, but the water seems to gleam the same insidious gold I saw in the pool at the Casa de Zafra. I hear a strange whisper, whether from the fountain or inside myself I can't tell.

Come to me.

Suddenly I know, deep in my being, that we are all in danger. I force myself to focus.

"Dad." I speak quickly, with the same sense of urgency that has saved me many times on a battlefield. "Whatever is calling to Marguerite and I from that fountain is dangerous. And not just for us. I think it is threatening for Mom, too. But whereas

Marguerite and I can protect ourselves in the pathways, or at least, navigate them, I think that if Mom somehow fell . . ."

But Dad has clearly heard enough. He is already moving into the Court. I can barely breathe for the heady pull of the fountain. My pendant throbs with an almost sexual pulse, the strange scent twining about my mind like a seduction.

Come to me.

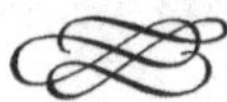

CHAPTER 16

WATER

Harper

ntoine and Aurelia are behind us, out of earshot. They linger by the dungeon, heads bent toward one another in conversation. Antoine must have begun telling her about his time here. It is typical of Antoine; now that his mind is made up to disclose all we know of the past, he won't want to waste any time.

I look at the two tall figures walking slowly toward us, faces grave and intent, and suppress a smile. *They are so very alike.*

Aurelia has all of Antoine's grim silence and stubborn determination, his sharp analytical mind and impatience to act. Watching Marguerite's eyes light up as she touches one of the ancient curlicued arches that surround the Court, I can admit that my younger daughter is equally like me. Marguerite lives as much in her imagination as she does in this world. It's why she's always fallen so easily into the water paths. Sometimes, over the years, I have wondered if it was her who carried me, when I was pregnant with the twins, into the water paths to my now dead sister Tessa, and to escape Keziah, who was trying to take me at the time. If it was Marguerite who fell into the water paths that day, it would have been Aurelia who acted to save me. My youngest daughter is governed entirely by intuition, my elder entirely by logic. As different as night and day, they are yet as bonded as Tessa and I ever were. *More, perhaps,* I think sadly, *given what they have endured together.*

"The Court of Lions is so called because of the fountain at the center." Marguerite moves across the marble flagstones of the courtyard to stand beside one of the marble lions that surround the fountain. Her hand rests lightly on the sculpture, almost in a caress. For some reason the gesture sends a tremor of unease through me. *It's just old paranoia about the girls being near water,* I tell myself. But the unease persists.

"Construction of the fountain began between 1362 and 1391, commissioned by the Nasrid sultan Muhammed V of the Emirate of Granada in Al-Andalus. It has undergone many reconstructions and modifications since then, including an overhaul of the hydraulic system beneath it." There's an odd gleam in Marguerite's eye as she speaks, and I notice her hand has paused on the lion. "The hydraulic system is extraordinarily sophisticated," she says quietly. "The Moorish skills with water transformed Spain's agricultural systems and persist to this day.

"Four water channels run from the base of this fountain, symbolizing the four rivers of paradise. Each of the twelve lions spout water into further channels which run across the marble courtyard, creating movement and sounds across the center of the palaces." She indicates the soft running channels, and her hand moves to the rim of the fountain. "There is a poem carved into the marble in Arabic, written by the poet Ibn Zamrak. The meaning of his words is hotly debated, but irrespective of his intention, the words are undeniably beautiful. My favorite line is this one." Her hand pauses atop the carved words.

"Its liquid silver goes over the daisies, melted and even purer.

Hard and soft are so close, that it would be hard to distinguish

Liquid and solid, marble and water. Which one is running?"

In the stillness of the courtyard her voice is quiet and intense. I realize I'm holding my breath, and when I glance around, I see the students are equally captivated. I notice Aurelia and Antoine emerging from the portico. Antoine's grim expression doesn't bode well. He's staring at the fountain like a threat he plans to take down, and my tremor of unease grows.

"Liquid silver," Marguerite repeats. "It is an interesting phrase to have used. Over the years, fanciful stories have grown over Zamrak's meaning. Some ambitious writers in earlier times, for example, thought that perhaps the fountain at one time had run with actual silver. It didn't, of course," she adds, to a ripple of laughter from her students. "But even modern engineers concede that those 14th century architects were masters of water."

Masters of water. The phrase sends a chill of fear down my spine. *What else,* I think, *did those masters of water understand, that my daughter is so obsessed with learning?*

Something tells me there is more to Marguerite's fascination with that fountain than simple history. And combined with our encounter with the nun, my unease is fast blowing out to full scale alarm.

"That's the tour." Marguerite inclines her head as the students applaud. "We'll talk about it in class on Monday. Meanwhile, enjoy the rest of your weekend." The students drift away into the gloaming, obeying the gestures of the guards ushering them to the exits. One of the guards calls to Marguerite in Spanish to be sure she's out before they do their final sweep. Marguerite nods in acknowledgment and he leaves. The Court of Lions is suddenly still, the chattering of the crowds gone, and as shadows gather in the corners, only the four of us remain.

"We should leave." Aurelia's face is as grim as Antoine's. She stares accusingly at Marguerite. "This isn't a good idea"—

"I just need to know." As Marguerite speaks, I hear an odd

sound, as if someone is talking, just out of earshot. I swing around, but there is nothing but shadows. And yet I can feel something, a familiar presence, one that sends a prickle of alarm through my skin.

"You can hear them, can't you?" Marguerite is staring at me, her face flushed with excitement. "The whispers. You can hear them, too."

CHAPTER 17

FOUNTAIN

Aurelia

arguerite's eyes are shining with excitement. "The whispers. You can hear them too."

I don't know about Mom, but I certainly can.

The whispers are not silvery snatches on the air, but a dull roar all around me, making the pendant pulse fiercely at my neck. The scent of pine and fir is rich, seductive, and tugging at me with a raw sexual ferocity that sings through my veins, pulling me onwards. The air gleams with golden danger and every nerve in my body is screaming that we need to leave, now. I take a deep breath, fighting for control. The twilight in the courtyard seems tinged with a strange, golden glow that prickles uneasily on my skin. Dad is examining the shadowy corners of the courtyard, his body stiff with tension, as if he, too, senses something lurking there. Mom is as tense as Dad, staring around the courtyard warily.

The tension I've felt in my body since the Casa de Zafra is rising like an inexorable tide. I suddenly feel furious at myself, and at my twin, for placing our parents in this position.

"Harper." Dad has crossed the courtyard in a preternatural instant, his hand gripping Mom's arm, locking her to his side just as she would have moved closer to the water. "Don't go near that fountain."

"Why?" Mom turns to him, then to Marguerite, confusion and concern warring with the savagery she barely ever allows us to see. "What is it you aren't telling me?"

Come to me.

The whisper is clearer now. A man's voice, hoarse and so close it sits inside my heart, calling to me like fate. That damned forest scent weaves a wave of lust and longing through my being so strong that I begin to ripple toward it, reaching into the waterpaths, desiring it despite my own deep knowledge of danger.

Come to me. There is a pain and longing in the words that reaches for me like the precipice in my dreams, drawing me forward, toward the abyss.

"Avery." My mother's whispered word reaches me as if from a great distance. A fierce bolt of pain cuts through the haze, arresting my fall. It forces me back into my material form, whilst also utterly weakening my ability to control that form. The pain permeates my every cell at once, hitting with such sudden ferocity that the world about me shimmers, wavering as if the pathways themselves have transcended their watery home and entered our physical reality.

Once I was in a hotel that had water running through a glass wall, so that everything on the other side was obscured, or distorted. That is how the courtyard appears to me now. Through the haze I see a tall, slender woman, with black curls that move around her face as if she were a mermaid underwater, and eyes that gleam the same strange, molten gold I saw at the Casa de Zafra, that has haunted my dreams for weeks now.

That deep, dangerous seam of gold is drawing my pendant

toward the woman, whilst also paralyzing me with a power I can barely breathe through.

"You promised us you wouldn't harm them." My father's voice is rough with fear and rage. "You promised Harper that our twins would never be in danger from you."

I can hear them speak, but I can't look at them. Marguerite is staring at the fountain, mesmerized by whatever it is that calls her. The water is running faster, trying to pull us in.

Come to me.

Marguerite's form is wavering, her being beginning to dissolve. The pendants at our necks are rising as they did back at the monastery, reaching for the gold in the woman's eyes. It feels as if that gold is tugging us both toward the waterpaths, but far more terrifying, I can sense the woman trying to get to our pendants—and vice versa.

She can't take Marguerite's. The thought strikes deadly fear within me. If Marguerite is lost in the waterpaths without her pendant, I know I will never find her. I force my body to edge in front of hers, blocking the woman's access to her, and I fight the fall with all my strength. I battle both the call of the man's voice, and the force pulling at the pendant. I am weakening, emotionally and physically, but I have spent my whole life training for war. I fight with all I have.

My body trembles with the effort to maintain my material form. It takes all my strength to force my hand to move up, trying to hold my pendant steady, whilst with my other I grip my twin's hand.

"Marguerite." I can barely speak; I'm only just hanging on, desperately trying to anchor my twin. Her pendant is gleaming ferociously, her whole body arching as she is drawn inexorably onwards, toward the woman, and the waterpaths.

Toward other worlds.

"No." My voice is breaking, just as I can feel my grip on her weakening. "Please, no."

But Marguerite stares past the roiling fountain water to fix on the strange, golden eyed woman. Despite her body already rippling into non-being with the pull of the waterpaths, she clutches my hand with a sudden, convulsive strength.

"Aurelia." I can't imagine the effort it has taken her to speak; Marguerite's form is indistinct, almost entirely dissolved. "We have to go," she whispers. "We have to go right now."

Even as she speaks, the woman leaps for us. Her golden, savage eyes are fixed on the pendants, both of which reach for her like a lover craving her touch. Vaguely I'm aware of our parents leaping to meet the woman, to get in between us, but I know in my heart they are too late. I hold desperately to Marguerite with one hand, trying to protect my pendant with the other; but I am too late.

The woman's hand closes over the chain as if it has closed over my heart. I muster every particle of my fading physical strength to combat her grip, trying to pull the pendant away from her. Time slows as we grapple, but I am no match for whatever supernatural force drives her. Nor can I fall into the waterpaths whilst also maintaining that material grip. Marguerite is rippling into oblivion, and I am the only thing holding her away from the other worlds I know are pulling at her.

Then the scent of pine and fir fills every cell of my being, darkly sensual, both terrifying and unbearably seductive. I'm vaguely aware of the woman screaming in pain, as some dark shadow behind her pulls her away from me. I feel a terrible, searing pain, and realize in horror it is the pendant being torn from my neck. My mother is reaching for me. I want to reach back, but I no longer have the physical form to do so.

Come to me.

I long for that voice, that presence, as much as both terrify me. I can sense the closed pathways opening, the man's voice like the key in the lock, summoning me beyond the precipice, toward the scented forest.

As the abyss reaches for me with rippling, shimmering light, my pendant flies out of the woman's hand and up, high into the air, turning slowly end over end as it tumbles back down.

My pendant hits the fountain, and shatters into a million shards of light, taking the world I know with it. I tumble over the precipice, and fall toward my fate.

CHAPTER 18

Harper

*A*very lunges forward, the perfect features twisted into an expression of fierce triumph, her eyes fixed on the pendant at Aurelia's neck. Antoine and I leap to meet her, to place ourselves between her and our daughters, but Avery is fast. Her hand closes over the chain as our daughters shimmer and ripple on the fading light.

I catch a glimpse of Aurelia's eyes, wide and terrified as she tries to hold on to her sister and fight the hand on the chain at her neck, and in a dreadful moment of clarity I know two things: that she can't do both; and that we won't reach Avery in time to help.

Avery had been a notorious beauty even before her transformation to immortal twenty-one years ago, but now she is simply extraordinary. Black curls snake around her face and her eyes gleam molten gold, cut through with preternatural flashes of turquoise. Her tall figure is slender and sylph like, her features perfectly symmetrical, skin smooth olive. Just as when I last saw her, on the dock of our mansion in Mississippi, there is a curious shifting nature to her presence, as if she is made of water itself, an illusion that could at any moment disappear. In an oddly detached moment, I wonder how she passes unnoticed through the world. I can't imagine anyone taking her for human.

For the second time that day, the girls pendants are glowing with that internal brilliance. They float upwards, toward the fountain.

Toward Avery.

The same blood that we believe lives inside the pendants runs through Avery's veins. It was what she used to transform herself into the creature she is now. We have feared the blood connection between her and the twins from the moment it was made. And now, despite her promises, it seems Avery is here to take advantage of it.

"Aurelia!" Marguerite's voice is no more than a whisper, her features oddly indistinct, as if part of her has already tumbled into the pathways. "We have to go. We have to go right now."

Then, from the dark recesses of the portico, a lean, snarling shadow leaps at Avery's neck, powerful jaws ripping into the perfect skin. Avery's face twists into a grimace of fury as she tries to hold onto the chain with one hand whilst fighting the wolf at her neck with the other, but despite the cracking of bones and terrible tearing of flesh, the animal holds on.

Antoine's face distorts into a killing rage as he reaches for Avery, the wolf still clinging to her neck. I grasp for my daughters, but my hands find only air.

Avery spins out of Antoine's grasp, her face twisted into a strange, chilling expression of triumph. I realize in horror that a broken chain dangles in her hand, whilst Aurelia's pendant spins up into the air overhead, above the fountain.

For a horrible moment it seems time stands still, as the small vial, the magic that anchors my twin girls to this life, to Antoine and me, spins end over end through the air. Avery shakes off the limp body of the wolf, sending it thudding dully to the tiled floor, and the three of us leap for it, Avery, Antoine, and I. But as if it has a life of its own, the pendant eludes us all, tumbling into the fountain water and smashing into a thousand pieces, turning the bubbling, seething water bright crimson.

Avery screams in rage and frustration. She ripples into translucence and is suddenly gone, seemingly disappearing into thin air. Antoine and I splash into the fountain, standing where our twins were only a moment ago. In place of their figures there is only the bubbling water, still colored crimson with the blood from Aurelia's pendant. I try futilely to gather the water in my hands but it slips through my fingers, the only means by which our eldest daughter might find her way back to us flowing away faster than I could ever contain it.

"Aurelia," I whisper, my voice breaking on the word. "Oh, my darling child. Where have you gone?"

I turn to Antoine, but he has left the fountain, and is crouched over the wolf lying on the marble tiles. There is nothing at all solicitous in his manner, however. He lifts the limp animal and shakes it, heedless of the broken bones and streaming blood. The wolf's body shimmers, already transforming back into the figure of a man.

"Guidry," Antoine says furiously. "Tell me where my daughters are, you bastard."

CHAPTER 19

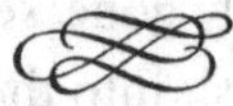

FALL

Aurelia

All around is crimson blood, and chaos.

The blood from my pendant surrounds me completely, seeping into my soul and the fragmented particles of my material body that exist in this space. The blood goes into me and through me, so I am utterly immersed. It hits like the atmosphere of an electrical storm, a shock of pure visceral power.

Even as I am held in and by the contents of my pendant, the loss of it leaves me feeling bereft, terrifyingly vulnerable. Flashes of insidious molten gold on the edge of my peripheral vision reach through the crimson mass toward us.

But my body is formless.

Without my pendant, I have no ability to navigate away from the gold reaching for me. Thankfully I still seem to be bound to Marguerite, energetically at least, as we are buffeted in the chaos. I can feel the gold reaching for us, trying to permeate the crimson darkness about me. The blood from my pendant feels oddly protective, like it is a shield holding us safe from the predatory gold seam. There is a savage triumph attached to that gold, a sense that something is closer than it has ever been to getting what it wants. Instinctively I want to fight it, but the gold pushes and directs me with a magnetic force I am powerless to resist.

Aurelia!

I sense rather than hear Marguerite at the same time that I feel her slipping away from me.

No! I reach for her mentally, but the anchor that has always bound us, the pendant at my neck, is gone. The feeling of being separated from my twin is crippling. Then the gold reaches for her, and crippling becomes terrifying.

In the disembodied mass I always am in this space, without my anchor, I cannot reach for my sister.

Come to me.

I cast my energy into the darkness, seeking the man's voice like it's my savior. Then I pause, uncertain if the voice is calling me toward the golden danger, or away from it.

Come to me.

This time the voice is stronger. I hear it just as the golden seam hits the edge of the crimson haze that surrounds me. Instinct tells me the voice and the gold are not connected. The gold moves and shifts like stained mercury, toxic and grasping. It feels like death. The voice calling me is visceral, sensual life, accompanied by the scent that has tortured me for years. It fills me with fear, not for my mortality, but for my sanity, for my body, for all the parts of me that I have sworn never to lose control of again.

It fills me with fear for my heart.

Come to me.

The voice calls me just as the gold seam stabs through the blood haze, breaking it's protective shield, sending the remnants of my pendant scattering. In a split moment of decision, I reach blindly through the dispersing crimson tide, trying to hold on to the voice, the scent, grasping for both in the turbulent void. But I find only the same closed pathways, the same labyrinth of mystery I always have. The gold comes closer, and I have a moment of resignation.

Whatever evil lives in those golden fragments will take me, and I will be lost here, in these pathways, forever.

Then comes a sudden blaze of white and aqua light, and the darkness clears, revealing an opening to the closed pathway I have sought for so long.

I reach for it energetically, tumbling headlong toward the whatever life awaits me at the end of it. The particles of my being knit themselves back together as the waterpaths thrust me back into the material world.

I'm lying face down on hard, rocky ground, and I smell war even before I open my eyes to the reality.

Fire and blood, but not that of modern warfare. I identify the crack of a Charleville 1777 musket, a sound so familiar to me from the years I spent traveling back to the American civil war that my heart skips a beat. I open my eyes cautiously.

I'm lying on a rocky hilltop, staring down at an alcazaba, a Spanish fortress. I know this one well; it lies about thirty miles north of Granada. There is a French tricolore flag flying from the ramparts. My heart stops momentarily, then begins beating again with a slow, excited pulse.

I made it through the closed pathways. I've traveled back to the 19th century. To Napoleonic Spain.

CHAPTER 20

KNIFE

Aurelia
Granada province, 1810

My heart thudding with mingled fear and excitement, I grasp for my pendant, even though I already know it is gone.

And with it, Marguerite.

A stab of sheer terror threatens to cripple me completely. Then a branch cracks behind me.

This is no time to indulge my emotions.

I tense but don't move. Grateful to discover my pack has survived the waterpaths, I slip my knife free, keeping my hand close to my side.

The soldier who moves into my range of vision dispels any lingering doubt as to where I am. He's wearing the navy blue coat and white underjacket of French infantry in 1810, and he's currently pointing his musket at me, an ugly smile on his face.

"*Señorita.*" His eyes roam over my body, though he keeps his musket up. I'm guessing I might not be the first Spanish woman he's met who has a knife hidden in her skirts.

However, I shouldn't imagine he's met any as adept with it as me. I stay down, keeping my eyes unfocused, as if I've been stunned.

It doesn't take much effort.

I've come out of the waterpaths in many strange locations. I'm accustomed to the shock and disorientation. But I've never had a journey like the one I've just endured.

And never once have I landed without my pendant. Without a way home.

But there's no time to think of any of that. The soldier is standing over me now. He nudges me onto my back with one worn black boot. I keep my body slack, rolling heavily with his movement. He smells of onions and wine, and his white breeches are covered in mud. He looks around, as if to satisfy himself that we're alone, and then he puts the musket down and reaches for the buttons at the front of his breeches. His eyes are glazed, and he's breathing heavily.

I wait until he's down on one knee reaching for my skirts before I slip my knife into his belly.

He dies easily enough.

I don't like killing, but I learned to get used to it a long time ago. And when it comes to men lifting my skirts on a battlefield, I don't hesitate. I've seen the mad heat of men after battle. Even in modern times, it isn't pretty. But the French soldiers who invaded Spain under Napoleon are particularly notable for their rape of both the land and women they conquered.

Who are *invading Spain.* I automatically change my manner of thinking as I roll away from the soldier and wipe my blade on the grass, looking about warily. I've always found it better to treat whatever time I find myself as the present, rather than the past. Experiencing the past as if it's some kind of exotic history immersion is dangerous. I've had a lifetime of landing in strange places, and learned to assess them immediately.

This battle is clearly all but over, and going by the tricolore flag and the lack of corpses wearing a French uniform, it seems Spanish resistance has been minimal. By the sounds of musket fire from the nearby streets, there is still some local fighting, but clearly the main body of the Spanish army abandoned their position soon after the French arrived.

I slip my knife into the sheath under my shawl. Staying down, I inch back toward the cover of nearby trees, looking about warily. I will have time to think about Marguerite, my pendant, and the fact that I'm finally in the one waterpath that has eluded me my whole life, when I'm safe. For now I need to get away from this battle. The town will be overrun with drunk soldiers long before sunset, going by the one I just encountered. That kind of nightmare I don't need.

My boots touch the tree trunk and I slowly uncurl myself to standing, slipping behind the tree as I do so. I take a step backwards and hit something almost as hard as the tree. A muscular forearm whips around my waist, and another comes over my chest, the hand covering my mouth.

Pine and fir. The smell of fate.

"*Dime quien eres,*" growls the voice that has haunted my dreams. *Tell me who you are.*

CHAPTER 21

WOLF

Antoine
Present day

I'm torn between the urge to kill the man I once thought of as brother, and the need to keep him alive purely for the information he might have.

"Antoine." The heartbreak in Harper's voice behind me adds fuel to my rage. "Don't hurt him. He's the only one who might know something."

"Then he'd better damned well start talking." I shake Guidry's naked form hard enough to break a few of the smaller bones. "Or I'll give that immortality a proper test."

"Go on, then." Guidry stares up at me from the marble tiles, his eyes full of pain deep enough to cut even through my rage. I remember when I first saw that darkness in his eyes, in the days after I was rescued from the Alhambra. I remember the way his eyes would slide away from mine as soon as I looked at him, the cavernous, aching grief that never truly left them again.

I had blamed myself back then. Many *guerilleros* had died

rescuing me. I knew one of them was a woman Guidry had loved.

But the two years of war prior to that time had kept us largely separated, me at sea, Guidry working for El Viajero on land. I did not know the men he had lost, nor the woman he had loved. Guidry never spoke of either. And I, filled with guilt at the price he had paid for my freedom, didn't raise the topic with him.

But that look in his eyes isn't one I will ever forget. Now it cuts through my rage, bringing with it a horrible suspicion.

"Which one?" My voice is little more than a broken rasp. I already know the answer to the question, though it breaks me to think of it. "Which one of my daughters did you fall in love with?"

Guidry's eyes meet mine, despite my hands currently being around his neck.

"Aurelia." There is a strange kind of wonder in the way he says the name. Slowly, savoring every syllable as if the name itself is forbidden fruit.

For a moment I truly believe I might kill him.

"You told me the woman you loved died." I can barely get the words out, rage and grief blurring the courtyard, and Guidry's face with it. All I can see is Aurelia's wide-eyed terror as she battled to hold onto her sister and her pendant before she disappeared. I shake Guidry so hard blood sprays across the tiles. "Tell me, you sly bastard. Did we just see our daughter for the last time?"

Harper makes a noise behind me like a wounded animal. I can feel her emotion crashing over me like a pulsating force. Even if I can restrain myself, Guidry won't ever make it out of this courtyard alive if Harper discovers our daughter is dead.

Once again Guidry does not look away from me, nor try to avoid the question. "I don't know," he says simply. "I know what happens to Aurelia directly after she falls into that fountain, and back to 1810, when I knew her. At least, I know some of it. But as to whether she makes it back to this time, or not. . ." His eyes shift between Harper and me. "From now on," he says quietly, "we are in the unknown future."

Harper and I stare at each with growing horror. My hands briefly tighten on Guidry's neck. "Then why didn't you save her? Save them both?" I slump down onto the tiles, though I keep hold of Guidry, afraid he will simply disappear again.

"Aurelia made me promise not to." Guidry stares back at me, the pain in his eyes as undeniable as the resignation in his voice. "Just as she made me promise never to speak of those years to you." He shakes his head. "Not that I could, even if I wanted to betray her faith. My tongue has been tied since the day I last saw her. A moment ago is the first time I have been able to so much as say her name aloud." His voice chokes on the last syllable and he looks away suddenly. I realize, with a sympathy I do not wish to feel, that he is overcome.

Two hundred years, I think reluctantly. *Two hundred years he has kept his silence and waited to see her again—and now she is gone.*

But the final part of that thought drives any trace sympathy away as fast as it came. Harper clearly feels the same lack of compassion, her eyes a blazing green fire as she stares down at Guidry's naked form.

"She made you promise not to." She makes a hard, furious sound. "And it never occurred to you to simply ignore that request? Or were you happy to wait two hundred years, just to send both of our daughters back to possible death?"

"You don't understand." Guidry twists from my grasp and comes to his feet. Striding across to the portico, he retrieves a bundle of clothes from behind a pillar and pulls them on, his back turned to us. "There's more at stake than even I know. To interfere today would have had far greater implications than you can begin to understand."

"What can possibly be more important than the lives of our

daughters?" Harper's face is still a picture of rage, her fists tightly clenched. "Are they together, at least, our girls? Can you tell us that much?"

"No." Guidry shakes his head, his back still turned to us. "I've never met Marguerite, other than catching a glimpse of her as a newborn infant. Today is the first time since the night the twins were born that I've laid eyes on her. Or on Aurelia, for that matter." Again his voice cracks on her name.

He swallows hard and turns back around, his eyes shifting between us. "I do know where Marguerite has gone," he says quietly. "And I can promise that you see her again. She will return here, to your time, later this year, although she will also leave again."

"And you know this how?" Harper's voice remains unforgiving.

"Because Aurelia and she remained connected." Guidry rubs a hand over his face, and I realize it's shaking at the same time I notice the blood seeping through his shirt, and the odd angle of his arm. In the distance I can hear the guard returning. There's nothing to be gained by being found here, especially given the mess of blood-stained water on the marble tiles.

"Come on, then," I say shortly. "There's no point in staying here. We can talk back at the house."

"Yes." Guidry nods. "And the others will be arriving, soon."

My eyes narrow. "What others? You mean Tate and Connor?"

"In part." Guidry half smiles. "Though there are others coming, too. Some you will remember, some not."

Suddenly impatient with all the mystery, I turn for the door, then back again, eyeing Guidry suspiciously. "Do I need to carry you there? Are you going to run again?"

"No." Guidry shakes his head, his half smile gone, the wracking grief back in his eyes. "No, Antoine. I'll be here now, so long as you tolerate my presence." He faces me again, squarely. "I wouldn't blame you if you couldn't." His eyes shift to Harper. "I wouldn't blame either of you."

Harper bares her teeth and hisses. "I'll listen to you," she spits. "But I won't forgive you for this, Guidry. Not ever."

Guidry nods slowly. "I know," he says, and the words are so heavy, so laden with the years he has carried them, that they fall into the air like stones on a pond. "I know you won't forgive me," he says. "Any more than I can forgive myself." He glances at me. "The guard is coming," he says quietly. "We should go."

He waits until I start to run, then follows behind me.

And though I curse the bastard to the furthest hell for what he has done to us, I can't help but feel a strange, unwelcome comfort at his familiar presence on my flank, and that thought feels like such a betrayal of my daughters that I run harder than I ever have, leaping the wall of that cursed palace and taking the rough hillside in long, furious strides.

CHAPTER 22

RAGE

Harper
Present Day

I run behind Guidry, keeping him in sight until the door of the carmen is closed behind us.

I don't trust him.

I also don't trust myself not to kill him.

It's ironic, really. In the years since he left us, I have always defended him to Antoine. I've argued there must have been a good reason for him leaving, and speculated, accurately as it turns out, that the waterpaths most likely rendered him unable to communicate.

But that was before I lost my daughters for the second time —with his foreknowledge.

Having him confirm what I have theorized over the years does nothing to help me understand, or forgive, him now. Before today, my anger at Guidry was more on Antoine's behalf, for the hurt that Guidry's betrayal caused him.

Now, however, I carry a mother's grief, and Guidry is the cause of it. I can't see past the red film of rage over my eyes. My hands tremble with a killing fury that takes every shred of my willpower to control.

You need to know everything he knows, I tell myself as I leap from the ground to the terrace. I can't be inside right now. I need the open air, and I need to have the Alhambra in my sight.

Some part of me harbors a faint, fluttering hope that my daughters may somehow reappear, as they have so many times before, barely an instant after they left.

Equally some primal instinct warns me that will not happen this time. The twins knew how terrified we would be at the manner of their departure. If they had been able to return, no matter how long they spent in the past, they would have done so, coming back here, to the house, if not to the courtyard of the Alhambra.

No. I know it in my soul. My girls are lost somewhere in the waterpaths, unable to get home.

My fingers clench the low wall of the terrace, hard enough to crumble the terracotta tile atop it. I watch the chips of tile fall uselessly to the cobblestones below, the red flecks like blood against the white walls.

"Harper." I don't turn at the sound of Antoine's voice. "You don't have to be here while I find out what he knows. If you'd rather not listen"—

"I will listen to every word that comes out of that damned wolf's mouth." I stare across the valley toward the Alhambra, still gripping the terrace wall. "And he'd better talk, Antoine. Or so help me, I'll kill the bastard myself."

"I'll help you do it." I spin around, my heart seizing as I see who the new voice belongs to.

"Connor!" I cross the terrace in a leap, throwing myself into my brother's arms. "Thank you," I whisper. "Thank you for coming back."

"We were coming anyway." Connor holds me tight, and I can sense him meeting Antoine's eyes behind my back. My brother and my husband will never be best friends, but they are family, and they are allies. Especially when it comes to me and the girls. I can feel their silent communication, and I draw a measure of comfort from it, especially when Tate's dark features appear behind Connor's back. I hug him wordlessly, then move to Iara, his tawny, round Venezuelan wife, and beautiful Cass, my dearest friend. Connor is an immortal wolf. Cass is a vampire, and a descendant of the Caribbean slaves who once cast earth magic to bind ancient vampires in Antoine's Mississippi mansion. Tate is Natchez, like Avery, and was as a brother to Antoine before they both became vampires. Iara, like Cass, is a younger vampire, turned during the same period we fought Keziah, twenty-one years ago. She is also my Maker, the one who drained me to death, then fed me her immortal blood. She is a part of me, just as is the old shaman Katiusca, who willingly gave his life to become part of me, the first mortal I drained to death.

But even Iara's presence is little comfort to me tonight. The circumstances are too horribly reminiscent of that night that I was made, the night my babies were born.

They are twenty-one years old, tonight, I think dully, as I stand in her arms. *I gave them up that night, sent them into the past to save their lives. Now, twenty-one years later, am I to lose them all over again? After all we went through to bring them safely into this world— and all we sacrificed to bring them back to us when we thought them lost to the waterpaths as babies?*

"We brought them back once before, Harper." Cass touches my arm. She must have read my mind, saying what I need to hear the most right now, as she always has. "We will do it again. You know none of us will give up until we do."

"What happened, exactly?" Tate asks Antoine. I turn away as Antoine briefly explains what we know.

"And Guidry knew it was going to happen?" Tate's question has an edge of incredulity. "All these years, he knew?"

"Not exactly, no, he didn't."

At the sound of Guidry's voice my fingers clench the terrace wall again, crumbling another tile into dust.

I can't look at him.

Cass and Iara, clearly sensing my fury, move to stand either side of me. Cass's tall, slender body is dark and cool beside me, Iara's warm and reassuring. Connor folds his arms and glares at Guidry, and even Tate's calm features wear an uncharacteristically savage expression.

Good.

I'm not the only one who has craved the chance to confront Guidry, over the years.

"Well then," says Connor coldly, "perhaps you might like to enlighten us with what you thought *would* happen."

Guidry is quiet for so long that eventually even I look at him. He is staring out at the Alhambra, the golden light from the palaces lighting the gaunt hollows and sharp planes of his face. He swallows convulsively. With a stab of sympathy that I bitterly resent, I realize that he's fighting to control his emotions.

"I thought," he says bleakly, "that she would come back."

When none of us look any less confused, he wipes a trembling hand over his face. "We didn't know what would happen back then, when she left." He is staring at Antoine. "She said—she told me—that if it was possible, she would come back here. Tonight." His voice breaks, and he turns his head away from us. "But she isn't here." His voice is so desolate it touches even me.

"Does that mean"—Antoine's voice is rough as old stone. He starts again. "Does that mean that they don't come back at all? Does it mean our daughters are—gone, forever?" I know he can't bear to say the word 'dead', and I'm glad. I can't hear that word. I think that if anyone utters it, I will break entirely.

Guidry shakes his head. "I don't know." He takes a deep breath and meets Antoine's eyes. "The truth is that Aurelia always believed it was unlikely she could return to this day. But she did believe there was another possibility. I hoped that she was wrong, but now, it is the only hope we have."

Clearly sensing our collective impatience with this prevarication, he hurries on.

"The other possibility, the one Aurelia believed, is that we now all exist on the same timeline, past and present at once. That the events back then are happening on the same days we are living them here, that the battles we fought back then, and that Marguerite fought elsewhere, are also being fought now, at this time." He shakes his head, one hand going behind his neck, frowning.

"I think you'd better start telling us where, exactly, our daughters are. Or rather, when." I take a deep breath and fight to keep my fury under control, but when I speak, I hear the hard, dangerous tone in my own voice. I can't help it. The rage is inside me, part of my nature, and my daughters are gone.

I won't apologize for it.

Guidry nods and turns to face me directly. "I first met Aurelia in January of 1810, about thirty miles from where we stand now. And Marguerite—" He pauses, as if searching for the right words.

"You've had two damned centuries to rehearse this conversation, and you still can't get it right." Antoine's cold anger matches my own. "But I think I already know the answer to that question." He turns to me, and I see my own fears mirrored in his eyes. "Marguerite isn't lost in time, Harper. She's lost in another world completely."

CHAPTER 23

ASTRIA

Harper
Present Day

"I'm right, aren't I?" Antoine folds his arms and glares at Guidry, who gives the slightest nod of his head. Antoine turns back to me. "Aurelia told me right before the girls disappeared. It's why I told you to get away from the fountain. It's also the reason Marguerite wanted us to visit it with her. She wanted to know if you heard the whispers from those other worlds, too."

"I did." I frown, remembering things I had been too disturbed to notice properly back in the courtyard. "I heard them just before everything started to happen. It was a strange sound, almost like a dozen radios all crackling at once. A cacophony of whispers, like a distant roar."

Tate nods. "That's how it was the night I went into the water paths with Jeremiah to bring the twins back when they were babies. It sounded exactly like that."

"Only these voices weren't only coming from times and places in history." Antoine turns back to me. "Aurelia finally told me the reason—or one of them, at least—that she and Marguerite hadn't been traveling a lot lately. And I honestly think the only reason she told me is because she was afraid that you might somehow be drawn into the paths yourself. She has a military mind." He frowns. "She saw a risk and decided to act."

"Yes." Guidry's voice sounds almost strangled, his eyes glistening. "That sounds like her."

My eyes narrow. "She didn't tell you this?"

He shakes his head slowly. "There was a lot she . . .couldn't say." His mouth tightens. "And even more that she wouldn't."

Antoine gives a hard cough of laughter. "Good for her." He turns back to me. "We know that certain pathways have always been closed to the girls."

I nod. "The French Revolution—or at least, since they were babies, and went there by accident." *And that was your fault, too.* I glare at Guidry, who doesn't avoid the accusation in my eyes. "Napoleonic Spain," I continue. "Regency England. And Marguerite told me recently that she can't travel to any of the major periods during which the Court of Lions was constructed or restored."

It's Guidry's turn to frown. "I didn't know that."

"Well," says Antoine acidly, "I'm pleased to hear there's something we know about our daughters that you don't." Guidry colors, and subsides. "It turns out," Antoine goes on, speaking directly to me, "that since childhood, there have been other pathways calling to Marguerite. Pathways Aurelia can't hear."

"Can't hear?" Iara leans forward. "Or can't sense altogether?"

"I don't know." Antoine passes a hand over his face. "There was no time. All she told me was that there are pathways Marguerite can hear that are completely closed to her. She can't follow Marguerite down them. And more than once, the girls have almost become lost when Marguerite began to fall into those pathways. You know she was never good at resisting the pull," he adds, speaking to me.

"Marguerite told me that she chose to study the Court of Lions for her dissertation because it was the one thing she couldn't actually visit in the past." I stare at Antoine, though it isn't his face I'm seeing, but Marguerite's, fragile and pale, her green eyes wide and luminous. "But what if it was because the Court of Lions is where she could hear those pathways most clearly?"

"If I might say something," says Guidry tentatively.

"Speak." I don't look at him. I'm still too furious, and not even the haunted look in his eyes or the gaunt, exhausted appearance of his rangy form can make me feel any better inclined toward him.

"Marguerite was drawn to those pathways because she is perhaps the only person on this earth able to navigate them. And because if she didn't, we would never have known about Astria—and about Anahita."

"Anahita?" *I remember that name.* "You mean Keziah's old ally, one of the three shamans who originally turned themselves into vampires?"

Guidry nods. "Yes."

"Keziah told me that Anahita was long gone. She hadn't felt her presence in centuries." I remember it as if it were yesterday. But I remember, too, the uncharacteristic note of uncertainty in Keziah's voice, the faint hesitancy in her words as she told me the story. "Keziah feared Anahita," I say slowly. "I think she was perhaps the only person Keziah was genuinely afraid of. Her, and the other shaman involved back then." I frown, trying to remember his name. "Darren—David?"

"Darien," says Guidry. "And there's a good reason Keziah was unsure. Anahita and Darien didn't die, or rather, they didn't cease to exist. They managed to leave this world and go into another one: Astria."

We all stare at him, the implications of what he's saying almost too big to truly contemplate. Around us the Granada night deepens, the full moon blazing over snow-covered mountains like a beacon, turning the them an almost iridescent white. A colony of bats fly overhead in a steady stream, their wings a soft rush on the spring air.

"So where is this Astria?" Antoine asks eventually, his voice hard. "And how do we get there?"

Guidry shakes his head. "You don't," he says, with a certainty that strikes terror into my heart.

"You mean that Aurelia tried?" I fear I already know the answer.

Guidry's eyes meet mine and flicker away, but not before I see the shadow of past fear that crosses them. "Yes," he says quietly. "She did. Many times."

"If she didn't succeed," Antoine says flatly, "how do you know anything about this other world? Or even that Marguerite made it there?"

"Because she and Aurelia managed to communicate. Not often, and it wasn't easy, but they could communicate. They worked together." His mouth tightens. "At least, they did back then. It's something to do with the Indigo in their blood." He turns to me. "Like you," he says quietly. "That was why Marguerite thought you might hear the Astrian waterpaths, even though Aurelia couldn't."

"But Aurelia has the same Indigo as her sister," I say.

Guidry lifts a shoulder. "I didn't say I understood it. I don't. I never did."

"Then Marguerite is somehow able to live in this other world. This . . .Astria."

"Yes." Guidry looks at me, his face shadowed. "Or at least, she did."

This time it's Connor who steps forward, his face dark with anger. "Stop talking around it," he says brusquely.

"When's the last time you heard anything from either of the girls?"

But it's Antoine and I that Guidry looks at when he answers. "The last time I saw Aurelia," he says quietly, was in 1812. She went back into the water paths to try to reunite with Marguerite, who still had a pendant that could bring them home. I don't know what happened to her after that—or whether she or Marguerite ever made it home."

CHAPTER 24

SCENT

Guidry
Granada province, 1810

"*C*uidado." *Careful.* Guidry tightens his arms around the woman, that damn scent filling his senses. He is terribly aware of his hand splayed over the flat plateau of her belly, the way her waist curves beneath his arm, the swell of her buttocks hard against him. For a man who has long since ceased to find novelty in his interactions with women, Guidry is deeply unsettled to discover that his mouth is oddly dry, and his body entirely aflame.

Christ. Mentally he tries to get a grip on himself. *You're little better than the French soldier she just killed.*

"*No tengas miedo.*" *Don't be afraid.* He waits until she nods cautiously against his hand before slowly relinquishing his hold on her, painfully aware of just how much he doesn't want to.

The woman, who is tall enough that her head rests just beneath Guidry's chin, raises her hands and turns slowly as he steps away. Her coloring is certainly Spanish, with creamy olive skin and a mass of black curls wound into a plait that hangs to her waist, though her eyes are a vivid cobalt rarely seen in the south. But the suede trousers, leather boots, and knife beneath her skirts speaks of a guerillero rather than the daughter of some rich *hidalgo*, with a duenna for chaperone. She regards him flatly, the rather determined planes of her face seemingly entirely unconcerned with the odd manner of their meeting.

Her eyes fall to the water flask at his hip and flare with need. *"Agua."* She mouths the word rather than speaking it, the urgency of her need apparent. Guidry hands her the flask, admiring her restraint when she forces herself to drink sparingly.

Guidry still doesn't know where she came from. One moment he was alone in the growing twilight; the next, a woman was lying on the ground barely feet from his hiding place. Before he'd so much as scrambled to his feet in surprise, she had slipped a knife into a French soldier with the kind of ruthless efficiency that even he, after a lifetime of killing, can't help but admire. Had he not been so astonished, he might have helped her do it. It was only when she backed into his body that he realized he was no longer imagining the scent that has haunted him so long.

The scent is coming from her. And he has absolutely no idea where she came from.

From the corner of his eye, Guidry notes a small group of French soldiers roaming toward them in the valley below. *Whoever she is, she's no ally of the French, if she's happy to stick one with a knife.*

"Los franceses están en todas partes," her murmurs as she hands the flask back. *The French are everywhere.* She nods again, her eyes surveying the landscape with the same kind of analytical assessment Lucia might. In a moment of decision Guidry is well aware he might live to regret, he gestures to the craggy mountains to the south. *"Primero corremos. Después hablamos." First we run. Then we talk.*

The woman nods. She begins to shuck off her skirts, then glances at Guidry with an almost guilty expression, as if she realized too late she was about to do something he might find shocking. Despite his own confusion and curiosity, Guidry fights the urge to smile. *"Si,"* he murmurs. *"Es mejor así."* Yes. *It's better this way.*

He turns studiously away as she tucks the skirts into a small leather satchel, thinking that he'd definitely have to run in front. If he has to follow those long, suede covered legs and the deliciously swelling buttocks, not to mention that tantalizing scent, he'll never find his way through the mountain paths.

Waiting until she's packed and ready, he sets off through the vineyards and olive groves surrounding the alcazaba, staying low to the ground and moving defensively until they reach the first undulations, and aren't so exposed. To his surprise, the woman copies his every move, and appears to keep pace with no discernible effort.

Vampire? Guidry dismisses the suspicion almost immediately. He'd been in close enough proximity to vampires throughout his existence to recognize the signs. There are no preternatural lights in the woman's eyes, nor the iron hard strength in her flesh that was impossible to disguise. Nor would a vampire have any need of a knife; the soldier would have simply been a hapless meal.

Wolf, then? He frowns as he runs, seeking evidence for this theory, but again, he comes up with nothing. He has always found it easy enough to recognize his own kind, even if he is aware his immortality sets him apart. Wolves have a certain scent, and an instinct that alerts them when a possible competitor is nearby. No. This woman isn't a wolf.

But she's something. Even the best trained female guerillero would have struggled to put a knife into that soldier with such practiced ease. Then there is the mystery of her abrupt appearance. Even if he had momentarily dozed off, which Guidry is quite certain he didn't, his wolfish senses would have alerted him to her presence long before she got that close to where he lay.

And then there is the small fact of her scent, which even now hovers around Guidry like an enchanted dream, stirring his body and clouding his thoughts.

He glances sideways as he rounds a curve on the hillside, catching a glimpse of her face. She's breathing easily, though still heavily enough to remove any trace of doubt that she might be either vampire or wolf, since neither would so much as pant at this point. But her face is set in a distant frown, as if she's lost in deep thought that has nothing to do with her present predicament. She runs with a trained ease that implies she's more than used to tackling high mountain paths. At night. With a stranger.

Guidry mentally shakes his head again. Even the most hardened guerillero women tend to move with companions, and at a slower pace. They might be as fiercely patriotic as their male counterparts, but few of them have any real combat experience, especially here in the south, where the French have only lately truly been a threat. Lucia is different; she actively went to war early on, gathering men loyal to her family, and those with the same ambitions, seeking out the French as far as she needed to roam to do so. But Lucia is an exception.

A spy, then. The unwelcome thought thuds into Guidry with enough heaviness to make him almost stumble. He is afraid of how much he doesn't want that to be true. But at the same time, he knows it is the first question Lucia will ask. One of their own dead is a small sacrifice if it will give the French eyes and ears inside the fiercest guerillero group in these mountains, and Lucia's band has already earned that reputation.

I can't lead her straight to the camp. Not until I know who she is. Feeling oddly like a traitor himself, Guidry forks right instead of left at the next turn, and leads them away from the finca, and toward a distant river.

He will find out who and what she is before leading her anywhere near the finca.

The dispatches will just have to wait.

CHAPTER 25

RUNNING

Aurelia
Granada province, 1810

My pendant is gone, and so is my sister.

I run through the growing Spanish night behind my new companion, trying and failing to make sense of what has happened.

Some things are clear enough.

From the moment the man's arm came around my waist, I knew I'd run into fate. After my initial relief that the absence of either brass buttons or a French accent meant the man was not a soldier, the sharp scent and gruff voice had been unmistakable.

Even worse, I hadn't been afraid.

Afraid? Ha! Be honest. My inner voice speaks up with a sardonic note I don't particularly appreciate. *If he hadn't stepped back to let you out of his arms, you might never have left them.*

I force the voice into temporary submission, and frown at the muscular back running in front of me. My captor is a rangy, lean young man with long, shaggy black hair, a vicious scar across his throat, and sloping hickory brown eyes far older than his face. His linen shirt is rolled to the elbow and open at the neck, loose wool trousers tied at the waist with a knife belt falling over soft boots. He doesn't wear a bandolier or carry a gun, but he does have a water flask, for which I'm still thankful. I'm still desperately thirsty. I always come out of the waterpaths in severe need of water, but I didn't want to raise the man's suspicions by taking too much of his. And my years in the military have taught me discipline when it comes to thirst, even if it cracks the back of my throat like fire on a summer's day. Oddly, however, my body feels almost uncannily strong. I normally come out of the waterpaths weak, crippled by thirst. This time, however, I feel as if I could run all night, and part of me wonders if it is the sheer exhilaration of finding myself in the company of the presence I've felt for so many years.

His is the face I saw at Casa de Zafra. I know it just as I know his is the scent that has haunted my dreams, his voice the one that summoned me.

Does he know what I am? But I discount that thought as soon as I have it. Going by the man's questions and caution, he clearly regards me with more than a little suspicion. *And yet his voice led me here.* I know it in my heart, though already, my logical mind begins to doubt my own instincts.

Perhaps it is coincidence. His voice is simply from this time. It was the fountain that brought me here, not some magical connection with a complete stranger. The mountain breeze cools my face as I run, carrying a maddening taste of the scent that has haunted me for so long. *Perhaps it was just these mountains I was smelling.* Except I've trained in these same mountains for years now. They smell of cypress, thyme, and summer grasses. The scent coming from my new companion is different, deeper, as if he he were sprung from a wilder, colder forest.

I shake my head impatiently. *After a lifetime trying to get here, you finally find yourself in 19th century Spain, and you're obsessing over the way a man smells?*

I draw on my years of training to detach, forcing myself to recount what I actually know so far.

I've studied every movement of French and Spanish forces, even the most minor skirmishes, and I know that the battle at the alcazaba took place in January of 1810. That means that barely days from now, the city of Granada will be occupied by the same French battalions we are running from.

I need to get to Granada before that. Despite all that has taken place, my military brain is still busily at work, assessing, calculating. It isn't by chance. I've trained myself, strictly and at times mercilessly, to operate rather than react. Before I knew how to walk, I knew I needed to find a way to manage what happened when Marguerite and I found ourselves lost in unknown places and times. I was a trained operative long before I formally entered the military.

And I've been training for this particular theatre of war since the first day my father said he had known Jeremiah back here, in this time, under the name El Viajero.

I am here. I'm not training anymore. This is real.

My mind, I realize, is dancing around and away from the facts I either can't understand, or can't bear to think of. I'm running behind a man who is both an absolute stranger in another time, and yet as familiar as my own being. I am following him into mountains known to be crawling with bands of guerilleros who are as notorious for their brutality as they are for their patriotism, and yet it does not even occur to me to distrust him. Nor can I so much as bear even the thought of running away from him. I feel connected, by a lifetime of intangible knowing, by all the things I have constantly denied myself feeling, to the rangy figure loping ahead of me. Running behind him feels at once like coming home, and also like running toward the very abyss I have always tried to avoid.

You don't even know his name. I try to thrust the unsettling feelings from my mind, but they do not leave, simply lurk beneath the surface.

My other thoughts are far darker, and harder to face.

I felt Marguerite spinning off into the darkness, away from me. More than that, I felt her sheer terror at whatever it was in the waterpaths trying to find us both. The insidious seam of gold that tried to penetrate the protective shield of the pendant's contents is the same energy that lived inside the woman who confronted us at the fountain. Even now I can feel them both, almost as if they live inside me. It is the darkest presence I've ever known, and I've felt strange things in the pathways over the years. The thought of Marguerite being taken by it still sends shockwaves of horror through my body now, as I race through the growing night behind my unknown companion. I remember sensing Marguerite's pendant leaving her body, and my knowledge that I had to stop that from happening. I knew it with a cold certainty that left no time for doubts or questions. I knew that if that pendant was gone, so would Marguerite be, forever.

But in that blinding moment, it was me and not my sister that the woman touched. My pendant, not hers, was taken. And it strikes me that I might have followed the wrong instincts. With my pendant, I could have gone into the paths, could have searched for her. But without it, how am I ever supposed to find her?

Even now I can see the strange flash of gold, feel the ice cold touch as my pendant was ripped away, not just from my physical form, but from my soul itself. *It was deliberate*, I think, running up the narrow mountain path behind the dark haired man. *It was taken, not lost.* Whatever drew us into the waterpaths back at the fountain came for our pendants. There is nothing random about what happened, either back at the Alhambra, or once we were inside the waterpaths. I instinctively know that we were taken deliberately, and for our pendants. But by what, or whom, I don't know.

And our parents know that woman. Mom had said her name: "Avery." And Dad had mentioned a promise she had made long ago, not to hurt us.

Anger and grief rip through me. Our parents know something about what is chasing us. If I'd only known the truth, perhaps I could better have protected Marguerite. Their knowledge that might have made the difference between me being lost with no way home, and Marguerite being lost in the waterpaths, perhaps in another world entirely.

Even though I managed to shield Marguerite from that attack, I hadn't been able to stop whatever that malevolent force is from taking my sister somewhere I can't follow. Somewhere I may never be able to follow, unless I can somehow find a way to get my pendant back.

But I am here. Despite the chaos of the day's events, I am finally in the one place where it might just be possible to find answers. Even, perhaps, another pendant.

Somewhere in Granada, at this very moment, Callie and Jeremiah are alive and well. Barely thirty miles from where I'm currently following an unknown man into a mountain fortress, live two people who can answer the questions my twin and I have been asking our entire lives.

If I can manage to stay alive, I think grimly, *and find my way to Granada before the French army does, I might just have a chance.*

It's a lot of uncertainty. But it's also a chance. And if my new companion is a guerillero, then he might just be the best chance I have of finding my way to El Viajero.

But he can't learn what you are, or who. I feel an odd twist of something like loneliness. The part of me that has woken a thousand times to that voice, to that disturbing scent, wants to throw myself into his arms and confide the whole.

But I'm here.

Despite everything that has taken place, and my crippling fear for Marguerite, I can't help but feel a certain exhilaration.

Finally, after all the years of speculation and failed attempts, my fate has called me. After the dreams and the longing, I am here, racing through the night behind the one person my body and soul have ached for, as long as I can remember.

Wonder and fear twine about my heart as I run through the smoke filled Spanish night, toward the unknown.

Toward El Viajero.

Toward my destiny.

CHAPTER 26

RESOLUTION

Antoine
Present Day

The gathering on the terrace breaks up soon after Guidry's bleak disclosures. There will be time for us to get the full story, but one look at Harper's face is enough to tell everyone that now is not that time. The others drift away, laying a comforting hand on my shoulder, an arm around Harper, but mostly their faces are just a blur.

Not again, I think, despair clawing at my insides. *Surely we can't have lost our daughters twice.* And this time there is no blood we can use to send someone into the waterpaths to find them. And even if there was, if Guidry is correct, none of us can follow where Marguerite gone.

My daughters are lost somewhere in worlds we can't enter, along pathways none of us can travel.

Harper lays her head on my shoulder, and I stroke her hair, taking comfort in her nearness, even if I feel helpless to alleviate her pain.

"They're truly lost this time," she says quietly. I nod against

134

her hair. I want to utter words of reassurance, but for once, I can't find them. "If they had made it home," Harper says, "they would be here now." I can hear the pain in her voice, the reluctance in the rasping heaviness.

"Remember what Guidry said." I reach for the only thread of hope I can find. "Marguerite will return to us, later this year. He said that Aurelia believed the girls were living the same timeline as us, which means that the last day Guidry saw Aurelia is still two years from now."

Harper pulls away and turns to face me, her brow creased. "Wait. How do you figure that?"

"Guidry said Aurelia thought we all might be on the same timeline now. If Aurelia has just landed in Napoleonic Spain, and assuming she met Guidry soon after her arrival, then it is currently January 1810." I stroke her hair back from her face. "We have until 1812 to change how this story ends, Harper. Time to find out as much as we can and work out how to bring our daughters home."

Harper's face is pale and drawn, but in the eyes I love so much, I can see the first stirring of something like hope, and it makes my heart ache. Strange preternatural iridescence flashes through the emerald green, the odd bolts of indigo that always lurk beneath my wife's extraordinary surface. "I didn't think of it like that," she breathes. "And Guidry did say we would see Marguerite again, didn't he?"

I nod, desperate to reassure her. "He did. And whatever else he might have done, I don't think Guidry would lie to us now."

Which doesn't make up for all the lies he told before, I think bitterly. All the years we had run side by side, fought together, drunk together. All that time, and never once had Guidry told me that he had loved my daughter.

Loved her, I think furiously, *and lost her, too.*

I can't forgive him for that subterfuge. I don't think I can ever forgive him, no matter what years of friendship have gone before.

"Antoine." Harper stares at me, her face suddenly animated. "What about me?"

If I had thought myself gripped by fear when my daughters disappeared before my eyes, now I feel the first stirrings of true terror. "What do you mean, what about you?"

But I already know what she means. I've known it since Aurelia first told me about the pathways leading to another world.

I'd just hoped Harper wouldn't connect the dots herself. Faint hope, of course. My wife is one of the most intelligent people I know.

"What if I can go into the waterpaths?" She says it now, throws it out in the open. "We know I did it before, when I was pregnant with the twins. And I could hear them, at the fountain. The whispers. I know we thought I couldn't travel the water paths after I became a vampire. But what if these pathways are different? Anahita and Darien navigated them, after all, and they are vampires. What if those pathways are different, and my Indigo blood can carry me through them, to Astria? To Marguerite?"

I can hear the hope in her voice, the tremulous excitement. I wish I could share it with her. But all I can feel is gnawing, horrible terror at the black, impossible prospect of losing not only my children, but my wife, the only woman I have ever truly loved. It is an abyss of loneliness I cannot bear to even contemplate, let alone discuss, and yet I also know that to ignore her suggestion will only make her more stubbornly pursue it.

I remain silent, trying to gather my thoughts, find the argument that will cut off this prospect.

"If it was you who heard those whispers," she says quietly, scrutinizing my face, "you would likely already be back at the

Alhambra, preparing to throw yourself into those pathways. Why is it any different for me?"

Because I can't lose you, too. Because my life has been lived, and I would sacrifice it tomorrow, if I went to my death knowing I had saved you, and my daughters.

"I won't throw my life away, Antoine." Harper reaches for my hand, and the understanding in her eyes splits my heart in two. "But nor will I stand by and do nothing if there is a chance I can save our children. I can't. And you can't ask it of me."

The night has stilled, the bats gone to their mountain home, the moon sliding down over the mountains. The Alhambra slumbers on the hill, its ethereal beauty hiding secrets that feel dark, terrible, and impossibly unknowable to me. I turn to Harper, and brush back a vivid auburn curl, twining the soft silk about my finger.

"I can't stop you," I say honestly, fighting to keep my voice even. "But I can ask you to wait. Until we know all Guidry does. Until we have had a chance to at least try to find other options." I cradle her face in my hands. "Will you give me that?" I ask, trying not to plead. "Will you just give it time?"

"Time." Harper makes a choked noise that might once have been laughter; but there is no laughter left to parents faced with the prospect of losing their children. "Time governs our lives, Antoine. Whether it's eternity, or the question of whether or not our girls are immortal. Time rules the life we live, and those to which our daughters travel. Yes, I will wait. For now. Until we know more. Until we've forced Guidry to tell us all he knows." Her eyes flash with a sudden, dangerous fury. "And he will tell us, Antoine. Even if I must torture every last word out of him."

I wince involuntarily. For a moment I am back there, in the Alhambra dungeons, Arkady's frankincense laced whip scourging the flesh from my bones, his poison forced down my throat, burning away my insides day after day, only for them to grow back and allow him another turn.

And along with that memory comes another: Guidry's face, leaning over me in that place as he wrapped me in a blanket, his horrified expression as he murmured: "You're safe now. You're safe."

And the days after that, when Guidry himself was lost in a bottle, eyes glazed dull with a loss he never spoke of, grief I knew haunted him for every decade of the two hundred years that followed.

Grief for my daughter.

And somehow, even despite all his deception, the years of lies, I cannot hate him.

But that doesn't mean I don't want to kill him.

You will need him now. Resolutely I thrust my anger aside. We can't do this without Guidry, and without what he knows. Whatever rage I feel toward the man who was once my friend, it will have to wait.

"Guidry will have his reckoning," I say to Harper. "I know it as surely as I do that we must find a way to bring our daughters home or die in the trying." She moves closer to me, her face turned up to mine, and I half smile. "Eternity might be a long time to hold a grudge," I say quietly, "but it also offers vast scope for punishment. Guidry has an immortal life. Either he helps us to get our daughters back, or I will ensure his eternity is one of dire misery. That I can promise you."

Harper looks up at me, and nods slowly. "But we will get them back."

It isn't a question. But nor is it a challenge I dare fail.

"We will," I say quietly. "We will bring our girls home, Harper. Or we will die trying."

Overhead a night hawk caws, and I watch it fly, across the valley and into the distant mountains, until its silhouette is lost.

EL VIAJERO

Granada, January 1810
Alexandre
(Jeremiah)

My dear Antoine,

It is late at night, and Granada is still cloaked in smoke from the explosion that almost cost you your life. You have just left my study, and, I hope, are now taking your rest in the bedroom above where I sit.

I doubt I will ever send this letter, nor any of the others I have written over the past two years. However, I will leave the letters, and the decision of what to do with them, to someone I trust entirely. I am a mortal man and will live a mortal life. It may be that at some point over the next two centuries, circumstances change, and permit my voice to reach you.

I cannot help but pray that happens. The agony you and Harper must feel at the loss of your daughters is unimaginable to me. To be unable to comfort you both has been the hardest silence I have ever kept, and I am a man well accustomed to silence.

I must say from the outset that these letters are written against the express wishes of your daughter Aurelia. She believes none of us can interfere with what is taking place in your time, without endangering you all.

But I know you and Harper. More than once I have seen you both work miracles when all has seemed lost. I cannot help but hope the same happens now.

Once, long ago, you wrote me a letter telling me that Guidry would one day come to my door. You told me that when it happened, I should trust him.

At the time, I loathed the man with the passion reserved for someone I considered a rival for the affections of my future wife. That is to say, the idea of trusting a man who had not only betrayed you, as I saw it, but also been the instrument by which Callie fell down the waterpaths into the past, was complete anathema.

And yet now, many years later, I am writing to ask the same of you that you once did me. If he lives still, then Guidry will recently have re-entered your life. I am asking you to trust him.

I understand that you have every reason to hate him. But Guidry loves your daughter, with a depth that still breaks my heart. Particularly today, when we all face the terrible prospect we may never see her again.

But I will not write things that strike more fear into your heart.

The simple truth is that I am an optimist by nature. I happen to believe that you do have a role to play in the coming days.

More importantly, I believe, very strongly, that you will see your daughters again. I need you and Harper to believe that too, Antoine. I need you to believe it with all your heart.

You and I both know that simply because something is intangible does not make it any less real. If this letter one day finds its way into your hands, we are communicating across time, and against all logic. That alone should tell you that anything is possible.

But none of it is possible if we do not believe. And I will add this: that the power of love, if you will forgive a much over worn phrase, has won over impossible odds a thousand times and more. I am trusting to love, now Antoine. The love you and Harper hold for your daughters. The love I hold for them.

Most of all, I am trusting in the love Guidry and Aurelia have for one another.

It is a rare and special gift, Antoine, one they have fought for time after time. To watch them these past years has humbled me, and touched me deeply. Please believe in them, and in yourselves.

For now, please take all the love Callie and I have to offer you, knowing that even if we cannot be at your side, that we are, most certainly, with you in our hearts.

Callie's name is now Therese, by the way. And mine, sent with my greatest affection, is

Alexandre Perrault.

∾

A Streak of Silver, the next in series, will be out soon. If you'd like to be the first to read and review new work, join Lucy Holden's ARC Team at www.lucyholden.com.

If you haven't done so already, download your other free Lucy Holden books on the same link.

Save over $20 on the Nightgarden Saga that precedes this prequel when you buy the discounted bundle. For only $9.99, receive the entire saga plus exclusive scenes, a prequel, and sequel.

Woven in Darkness, the first book set in the world Marguerite has fallen into, is out now on Amazon.